Hard SIN

the alpha antihero series

SYBIL BARTEL

Copyright © 2020 by Sybil Bartel

Cover art by: CT Cover Creations, www.ctcovercreations.com
Cover photo by: Wander Aguiar, wanderaguiar.com
Cover Model: Kaz van der Waard
Edited by: Hot Tree Editing, www.hottreeediting.com
Formatting by: Champagne Book Design

All rights reserved. No part of this publication may be reproduced, distributed, or transmitted in any form or by any means, including photocopying, recording, or other electronic or mechanical methods, without the prior written permission of the author, except in the case of brief quotations embodied in critical reviews and certain other noncommercial uses permitted by copyright law.

All characters in this book have no existence outside the imagination of the author and have no relation whatsoever to anyone bearing the same name or names. They are not even distantly inspired by any individual known or unknown to the author, and all incidents are pure invention.

Warning: This book contains offensive language, alpha males and graphic sexual situations that may be difficult for some audiences. Mature audiences only. 18+

Books by
SYBIL BARTEL

The Alpha Antihero Series
HARD LIMIT
HARD JUSTICE
HARD SIN
HARD TRUTH

The Uncompromising Series
TALON
NEIL
ANDRÉ
BENNETT
CALLAN

The Alpha Bodyguard Series
SCANDALOUS
MERCILESS
RECKLESS
RUTHLESS
FEARLESS
CALLOUS
RELENTLESS
SHAMELESS

The Alpha Escort Series
THRUST
ROUGH
GRIND

The Unchecked Series
IMPOSSIBLE PROMISE
IMPOSSIBLE CHOICE
IMPOSSIBLE END

The Rock Harder Series
NO APOLOGIES

Join Sybil Bartel's Mailing List to get the news first on her upcoming releases, giveaways and exclusive excerpts! You'll also get a FREE book for joining!

the alpha antihero series

My childhood stolen.

My future robbed.

My life had been hijacked since before I was born.

Every day I woke with air in my lungs was a reminder of what I'd lost. But I didn't escape the most violent cult in the country and survive four tours in the Army to go down like this.

I was Candle Scott, and this was war.

*HARD SIN is the third book in the Alpha Antihero Series, and it is not a standalone story.

The Alpha Antihero Series:
HARD LIMIT
HARD JUSTICE
HARD SIN
HARD TRUTH

For Mom and Dad

"Candle was earth. Dark and dirty between your hands, he rubbed across your skin and left marks as his scent soaked into you like a memory. You smelled him after every rain, and you felt him every time you fell. He'd cradle you if you needed to lie down in the woods, but he'd never lift you up to touch the stars."

—Kendall, from ANDRÉ

Chapter ONE

Candle
Camp Leatherneck
Helmand Province, Afghanistan.

Hot, dusty, and tired as fuck, my eyes were closed before my back hit the bunk.

"Not so fast, Sarge. Don't fall asleep yet. Lieutenant wants to see you."

I opened one eye to look at my gunner. I was five minutes off a three-day combat mission that should've taken two hours, but the goddamn HVT had evaded us because all our intel had been bad. I hadn't slept since… fuck, Thursday night, I thought.

"Is it Monday?" Four years out of that hellhole compound in the Florida Everglades and everything in my life was different, but I still didn't keep track of the days of the week.

"Yep." My gunner, Leeds, glanced at his watch. "Monday, the seventeenth. Eleven hundred hours."

Not giving a shit what day of the month it was any more

than what day of the week it was, I swung my boots off one of the dusty, stained mattresses that every soldier on base except me complained about. The bed was more comfortable than anything I'd slept on growing up.

"What does the LT want?" We'd already debriefed.

"No clue, Sarge, but he said it was urgent."

"Copy that." Not fucking thrilled, I hauled my ass up. If I didn't get at least four hours of sleep, I'd be useless behind my scope. I'd volunteered for enough back-to-back missions to know my limit. Sleep deprivation kicked my ass on day four, which was two days longer than most men in my unit. My eyes wanting to close even though my body was upright and moving, I aimed for the door of the tent that served as our barracks.

Leeds followed me outside. "Dawson and Roberts said there's another mission."

The hot Afghan sun didn't swamp you like Florida sun, it stole your fucking breath.

"There's always another mission." I lowered a pair of sunglasses I hadn't bothered taking off before I hit my bunk and walked toward the LT's quarters. Leeds still on my heels, I glanced at him. "You get called in too?"

"No," he admitted. "But if it's another mission, I figure I'll let the rest of the team know."

Leeds had slept twice by my count while we'd been out on the mission. Next to Doc, he was the man you didn't want fucking up his job because he was too damn tired to hold his eyes open. "How many of those caffeine pills you take since last night?" I hated the fucking things.

"Eight, why?"

Jesus fucking Christ. "Go get some sleep. I'll come get you if there's anything you need to know before sundown."

"I'm not tired. I'm good."

"Not a request, Leeds."

"You sure, Sarge? Because I could—"

"Leave. Now."

He opened his mouth to protest, but a Chinook flew overhead, drowning him out.

Not waiting to see what the fuck he had to say, I shoved my sunglasses up and walked into my LT's quarters. "Lieutenant, you wanted to see me?" Hands behind my back, feet shoulder width, I stared straight ahead.

Standing behind his desk, Lieutenant Hoskins eyed me a moment. "How long have I known you, Scott?"

Learning the difference between a rhetorical question and an actual question took me years. This one was both. "A while, sir." I gave the safe answer because I didn't count years any more than I counted days.

"That's right, since you got out of Ranger school. Four years. So tell me, how the hell did I not know you're married?"

One word, and every muscle in my body went rigid.

Married.

My blood ran cold, and the sleep deprivation took a back seat. Like a fucking psychotic break, my left palm, the one I always held the small carved wood piece in, itched.

If I'd learned one thing above all else in this shithole of a world, I'd learned silence was powerful.

So I didn't utter a word.

The lieutenant raised his eyebrow. "You're not going to say anything?"

"I'll say whatever you want me to say, sir." Because I didn't know what the fuck this was about, and I sure as hell wasn't going to tip my hand about anything pertaining to my past. I kept that shit under lock and key. No one except that recruiter four years ago, the FBI agent, Morrison, and Stone Hawkins knew who I was.

Hawkins wouldn't say shit to anyone, the recruiter was ordered not to, and the FBI agent, well, my money was on him being behind whatever the hell was going on.

The lieutenant snorted as he shoved papers around on his desk. "Right. Of course you will, because you're the cagiest fucker I've ever served with." He looked up. "Also the most relentless." His hard gaze pinned on me, he pushed a paper across his desk. "Your wife needs you. Go take care of whatever you have going on. Transport is already here. They'll get you to Germany, then you're on a civilian flight to Florida. I'm told your father will meet you at the airport."

I took the paper and nodded, but I didn't read it. I didn't even look at it. I could read now, barely, but I knew it wouldn't matter what words I'd discern from the damn thing. Whatever excuse was getting me sent stateside was a lie.

The lieutenant eyed me a moment longer, then he shook his head. "You got a week. Then get back here. We already have our next mission. Dismissed."

I saluted, then pivoted and walked to the door.

"Sergeant," he clipped.

I glanced back. "Sir?"

His shrewd gaze held mine. "Personally, I don't give a fuck where you come from or what goes on in your private life. I care whether or not you can do the job, and you deliver.

Always have. You don't play by the rules. We both know that. We also both know I selectively look the other way when I need to because you're one of the best Rangers I've ever met."

"Thank you, sir." I didn't give a shit about being the best. I gave a shit about learning every tactical advantage I could.

"That said..." Nodding at the paper in my hand, he continued as if I'd said nothing. "I've never had something like this come across my desk in all my years in the service. The Army doesn't grant Rangers leave because his wife needs her hand held for something. So I'm going to ask you a question once, off the record, man to man." He dropped his usual guarded expression. "Is this something I need to be concerned about?"

"No." I intentionally didn't say sir.

"You even got a wife?"

The question hit me in the chest and robbed the fucking air from my lungs right before the rage set in, but I didn't so much as blink. "I did. Once." It didn't matter that we'd never gotten any formal paperwork. My woman had been mine in every sense and every way.

The lieutenant nodded slowly. "And now?"

My jaw ticked, my hands fisted, and I thought about lying. If I'd slept in the past few days, I probably would have. But the memory of my woman's strawberry-blonde hair and green eyes cursed my existence, and suddenly I wanted to believe this discussion truly was off the record because I hadn't had a real fucking conversation in four years.

Or maybe I just selfishly wanted to tell someone about her. She deserved that. She deserved to have her memory on the tallest fucking pedestal there was, because she was the purest person I'd ever known. But I never told anyone about her. I kept her memory locked up tight where she was both my salvation and damnation. She was dead, and I didn't deserve to be alive, but life was never fucking fair.

I ground out two words. "She's deceased."

A split second of compassion crossed the lieutenant's face before he shut it down. "And your father? Is that who's really going to be waiting for you stateside?"

"I don't have a father." A con man and a fucking sociopath, River Stephens had never been my father, nor would it be him waiting for me at the airport, because he never left River Ranch.

"You someone special?" he asked. "A senator's kid or something?"

"No."

The lieutenant frowned. "You getting recruited by Counterintelligence?"

Definitely not. "I'm just a Ranger."

He didn't look impressed. "That piece of paper in your hand says you're a hell of a lot more. Someone high up is pulling strings for you."

"More likely pulling strings around me."

The lieutenant's eyebrows shot up. "You in trouble?"

"Nothing I can't handle." Whatever it was.

"You sure about that?"

"No," I answered honestly.

The lieutenant exhaled. "All right. I'm done asking, because frankly, I don't want to know any more. But there's a guy, a Marine I served with, and you can trust him. He recently got out and started his own security firm in Florida. Name's André Luna." He opened his desk drawer and pulled out a cell phone. "Luna and Associates is his company, and he's in Miami. You get in trouble, look him up and call him. Tell him I vouch for you." He slid the phone across the desk to me. "This cell is untraceable."

I took the phone and memorized the name. "Thank you, sir."

He eyed me a moment. Then he nodded to himself as if making a decision. "If you get in serious trouble, Luna has a buddy. Corpsman who served with Luna's unit. Guy by the name of Talon Talerco. He's crazy as shit, but I never saw a better combat medic. He's in Daytona Beach, and rumor has it he owns a surf shop now. Look him up if you need him. He'll know my name."

"Copy that." I acknowledged him out of respect, but I wasn't going to call either of them.

My LT tipped his chin toward the door. "Get out of here before you miss your transport."

"Yes, sir."

Chapter TWO

Candle
Twenty-Two Hours Later
Miami, Florida

Itching to stretch my legs, I looked out the window at miles of pavement with palm trees in the distance. The plane taxied to the gate, and I waited until the red seat belt sign turned off before I got up from the first class seat I'd been upgraded to.

Standing out in my ACU, beret, and dusty combat boots, I grabbed my rucksack out of the overhead bin.

A blonde flight attendant who'd been trying to get my attention every time I opened my damn eyes on the twelve-hour flight stepped around another passenger to get to me. "Thank you for your service, Sergeant." With a face full of makeup, she smiled and dropped her voice as she slid a piece of paper into my hand. "I'll be in Miami for twenty-four hours. Call me."

I grabbed her wrist and leaned down to her ear. "Even if I was here for pleasure, which I'm not, I wouldn't call you.

If you'd wanted to get on your knees and suck my dick midflight, I wouldn't have said no." Standing to my full height, I shoved the paper back at her. "But that opportunity's passed. Keep this for the next uniformed guy you throw yourself at."

I didn't wait to see if I got slapped in the face. I walked off the plane.

Two paces past the jetway, my suspicion was confirmed.

FBI Agent Tom Morrison stood with his hands on his hips as he nodded at me. "Scott."

"Morrison."

"Thanks for coming."

Prick. "Did I have a choice?"

His hair more gray, his eyes tired, his middle larger, he almost smiled. "Not the way I arranged it." He tipped his chin toward the exit. "This way. I'm parked in a red zone."

I echoed my lieutenant's sentiment. "You must have some kind of pull."

This time Morrison did smile, but he also shook his head. "Used every favor I ever accumulated in my entire career to get you here."

"Hope it's worth it."

"Me too," he mused. "Me too."

I didn't ask why I was here, and he didn't offer any more information.

I followed him to his car and got in the passenger seat. It was a different vehicle than the last time I'd ridden with him, but the smell was the same as I'd remembered—sweat and old food.

Once he was behind the wheel, he glanced at my arms

before pulling out into traffic. "You look good. Got some tattoos, I see."

None that weren't relevant. "Why am I here?" I hadn't been back to Florida since I'd been hauled off to basic training.

The agent rubbed his chin. "River Stephens is still alive, if that's what you were wondering."

"I wasn't." I knew ATF had recently raided the compound and a shit ton of members were dead, probably shot by other members, but River had escaped capture. "I know he's still free."

I'd struck a deal with Morrison before I'd enlisted. He'd promised to get word to me if they ever got the fucker. Which they wouldn't, not unless they were willing to kill three hundred people, half of which were women and children, just to get to Stephens, because that was the kind of sick fuck River was. He'd make every cult member surround him and die for him if it came to that. I'd heard about the massive casualties in the news from the last raid, but they still hadn't caught the motherfucker.

"Yeah," Morrison acknowledged quietly. "He's still out there."

"Shocker."

Morrison looked at me like he didn't know if I was being serious or not. Clearing his throat, he brought his gaze back to the road and changed the subject. "Looks like the military's been good to you."

I'd spent the first months in the Army suffocating in rage and grief. Then Ranger school broke me down and rebuilt me. I wasn't the naïve, trigger-pulling, ignorant fuck I was four years ago. Now I was a calculating, lethal killer, and I finally had a plan.

A simple fucking plan.

Military assault rifles. Illegal in the States. River Stephens didn't have them, and I could guarantee he'd want them. So would Stone Hawkins. I had a contact in Afghanistan who was working on getting me Israeli Tavors. Once I had them stateside, I'd let both River and Stone know they were for sale. River wouldn't miss an opportunity to make an example out of me, and Stone wouldn't pass up a chance to double-cross someone like River. The plan was brilliant in its simplicity. Then I'd set a meet in front of the compound gates and kill them both.

After that, I could care fuck-all about what kind of evidence Stone Hawkins kept on me. I'd gladly go to jail for killing those bikers four years ago. Prison would be a cakewalk compared to growing up in River Ranch.

Except I didn't intend on getting caught, let alone going to prison. The last part of my plan was to disappear into the Glades where no one would find me and live the rest of my life being left the fuck alone.

Which led me back to the present and why the hell Morrison had brought me here.

"I'm tired of asking why I'm here, Morrison, and I'm not in the mood for small talk. I need to get back to my squad. How long is this going to take?" I had no intention of being stateside for a week. I had shit to do downrange.

"Well," Morrison hedged. "I think how long this takes is going to be up to you."

I hated games. I hated people who played them even

more. I didn't remember Morrison being a prick when I'd dealt with him before, but I guess shit changed. "What the hell does that mean?"

A half smile hit his face. "I see the Rangers have worn off on you."

"Your point?"

"You talk different."

I thought different. I shot different. I killed different. None of which I was going to discuss with him. "I'm giving you twenty-four hours." Two of those hours he could have me awake. The rest I was going to sleep in a bed somewhere without the sound of fucking war around me.

"I can work with that." He pulled into an underground garage of a residential-looking building.

I'd seen downtown Miami exactly twice—once on my way to basic training and now. It was enough for me to know I hated it here. "I don't give a shit what you can work with. The sooner I get out of here, the better."

He pulled into a parking space and looked at me. "Is it Miami that's making you edgy, or are you anxious to get back to Afghanistan?"

There was no way to answer his question without divulging personal information, and I didn't give shit away about myself. Not anymore. Not after the last time I handed him my background on a silver platter and my woman wound up dead a few hours later.

Ignoring his question, feeling naked without my rifle in my hand, I undid my seat belt. "Where are we going?"

"Upstairs."

"You live here?" I pushed open my door with too

much force, because it was lighter than any door on the armor-plated Humvees downrange. Feeling exposed, I stepped out of the car and scanned the garage.

Morrison laughed without humor. "This zip code isn't in my pay grade." He looked at me over the roof of the car. "Speaking of money, you never changed the address on that bank account I set up for you. I still get the paper statements."

Four years ago, after I'd shown back up at the recruiter's with blood all over my shirt, Morrison had told me he was sorry for my loss. Then in the next breath, he'd said he'd secured a monetary reward for the information I'd given him on River Ranch and River Stephens. I hadn't said shit.

In fact, I hadn't said anything that day after I told him my woman was dead, except that I needed to get into the Army immediately. Morrison had taken it upon himself to set me up with a bank account for the reward money and told me to switch the mailing address when I knew what mine would be.

I never did.

I didn't want blood money. I wanted my woman back, but that wasn't fucking happening.

"Scott?"

Anger I kept carefully controlled seeped through the cracks. "What?"

Morrison looked at me like he was trying to solve a puzzle. "Have you even touched that account?"

"No."

He let out an exhale. "That's a lot of money to leave sitting around."

I didn't give a shit about money, except how much I

needed to buy the fenced weapons. "You gonna tell me the reason I'm here?"

He stared at me a moment. "I'm going to show you. Come on. Elevator's over here."

I preferred stairs, but I didn't comment.

We took the elevator up twelve floors, then we walked down a long hall. Every step further I took, instinct kicked up until adrenaline was pounding in my veins like I was down-range on a combat mission with an HVT in my sights.

"Who's here?" I demanded of Morrison as he shoved a key into the last door in the hallway.

He didn't reply.

Instead, he pushed the door open, then tipped his chin for me to enter.

Muscles primed, fists ready, every technique in hand-to-hand combat I'd been taught running through my head, I walked into the small apartment.

Then I stopped dead in my tracks.

Looking scared as fuck, her arm cut all to hell, she sat on a couch in a goddamn compound dress.

Shock robbed the authority from my voice. "Decima?"

"*Tarquin?*" she whispered in disbelief.

Chapter

THREE

Candle

> "Take the offer, Decima." Jesus fucking Christ. *"Take the offer."* Two goddamn hours I'd been trying to convince her to take the deal the Feds were offering, but she was more stubborn than my woman had been. "The U.S. Marshals will relocate you, and you'll be safe. You'll get a new life."

Resolutely refusing, she shook her head for the hundredth time. "I will not go with them." Holding my gaze, her eyes pleaded. "But I will go with you."

"You can't come with me. I'm deployed to a war zone." Christ. "I've explained all this to you."

"I will wait for you then."

Out of patience, I thought about what my lieutenant had said. André Luna and Talon Talerco. One with a security firm and the means to protect her, but he was local. And I wasn't going to leave her somewhere Stone Hawkins could find her. That left the second option my lieutenant had mentioned.

An idea formed.

"Stay here," I ordered Decima before getting up and walking to the small kitchen where Morrison was sitting with some ATF fuck. "Morrison, I need to talk to you. In private." I didn't wait for a response. I walked out of the apartment and into the hall.

A moment later, Morrison followed. "What's up?"

"If I set her up in a place, will you check on her at first, until she gets her bearings?"

Morrison frowned. "The Marshals should handle this. She'll be much safer in WITSEC."

"She'll run before she'll agree to that." I knew fuck all about her, but five minutes in her presence and I knew that much.

Morrison sighed heavily. "What are you thinking?"

"How much is a house on the beach in Daytona?" My woman had wanted a house on the beach. That Talerco guy was in Daytona. Daytona seemed as good a place as any to land when I got out of the Army, and it wasn't close to Miami.

Morrison snorted. "More than you got."

"I have more than what you put in that bank account for me." Saving up for black market assault rifles, I hadn't spent any of my salary.

Morrison's eyebrows shot up. "You're serious?"

I didn't say shit. Of course I was serious.

He muttered a curse.

I waited.

He sighed. "Daytona? Really? That's a drive from Miami."

Hard SIN

"She won't need checking on often." I had a feeling Decima would figure shit out a hell of a lot faster than I did. "I just need to get her into a place today."

His hands went to his hips as his shoulders sagged in defeat. "Come on, Scott. I brought you here because I thought you could talk some sense into her. Get her into WITSEC, and get her to tell us everything she knows, not just the generalities. I didn't expect you to come in and play the knight on a white horse." He let out a short laugh void of humor. "But I should've known." He shook his head. "Word is you're unstoppable. Fastest Ranger to ever climb the ranks. You volunteer for every damn mission."

I didn't touch his last statements. "You brought me here because you feel sorry for her, just like you felt sorry for me four years ago." I could see it in his eyes. "If you told her to tell you what she knows, then she's already given everything she has. She's a River Ranch female, she's submissive and she'll do what she's told."

"Except go into witness protection," Morrison corrected.

"She's scared, and she doesn't trust you. Help me find a place in Daytona, preferably furnished. Make some calls, do what you have to do. Let's get this wrapped up. She'll also need an ID." I made up a name on the spot. "Kendall Reed is her new name." My lieutenant's first name was Ken and Reed Jenkins was another Ranger I respected. "And get her some normal clothes, for fuck's sake." I didn't wait to hear him bitch. I walked back into the apartment.

Decima hadn't moved an inch.

I sat down next to her. "Here's the deal if you don't want to go into witness protection. Your new name will be Kendall

Reed. I'll put you up in a place in Daytona Beach, and you'll be on your own when I'm deployed."

Her hands twisted in her lap. "And when you are not deployed?"

"I'll be home." The last word left a bitter taste in my mouth.

I didn't have a fucking home. I never would. Not the one I wanted. Not the one my woman had wanted. And I didn't want to live in Daytona any more than I wanted to live in Miami, but it was the lesser of two evils, and I felt like I owed her. The least I could do was give her a place to stay while she adjusted to life outside the compound. I could hold off on disappearing into the Glades until she was on her feet.

"What will I do?" she asked tentatively.

"Cook your own meals, get a job, adjust." I didn't give a shit what she did. I didn't want to fuck her, and I didn't want to look at her in the goddamn compound dress. All she did was remind me of the past, which was why I both couldn't stand her and couldn't walk away from her.

"Okay." She nodded. "I can do that."

The agent walked into the living room with his phone to his ear. Looking at me, he lifted an eyebrow. "Ormond Beach, place is practically on the sand. You can afford it. That work?"

I didn't know where the hell Ormond Beach was. All I knew was that it wasn't Miami. "Yeah. Make it happen."

Chapter
FOUR

Candle
Two days later
Ormond Beach, Florida

Drinking coffee I made myself, I looked out the kitchen window at the view of the beach.

Morrison had come through.

Someone he worked with had recently inherited this two-bedroom beach bungalow from a deceased relative. The place needed work, but it was furnished and it was now mine.

I was a fucking home owner.

Nothing I ever would've thought about if it weren't for my woman. Her memory still sharp in my chest, I didn't notice Decima come up behind me.

"You should have woken me. I would have made you coffee."

"No need. I did it myself." Another thing the Army had taught me.

"I am sorry I overslept."

I turned and took in the too-big T-shirt she wore over a pair of men's sweats. Some fucking clothes Morrison had gotten her. "Don't apologize to me for shit. We'll get you clothes today."

Her head bent, her long hair hanging over her face, she fingered the hem of her shirt. "Or… I could take it off."

Fuck.

I knew this was coming.

Tamping down my temper, I put enough force into my tone so she'd know I meant business. "You'll leave it on."

She didn't look up at me, and she didn't let go of the hem of the shirt. "It has been two days since I have been in your house," she replied quietly, submissively.

I knew how long it was. I was in the same damn car when Morrison drove us up here and handed me the keys.

"Your point?" I knew her point. She saw herself as my property now. "I told you two nights ago, I'm not fucking you." It was the first goddamn thing I'd said to her the second Morrison took off, leaving us alone. "I'm not ever gonna fuck you." She was my past, and I didn't fuck my past. I didn't fuck, period. Four goddamn years and I hadn't fucked a woman. My cock hadn't touched pussy since the day my woman took her last breath.

Yeah, I'd fucked around. I'd had my dick sucked by a handful of women, but I'd never fucked any of them.

I couldn't.

I'd been kicked out of River Ranch, but there was one goddamn part of me that had never left.

And this was it. Right here. This exact fucking scenario.

I couldn't fuck Decima.

I wouldn't.

I wouldn't fuck her or any other woman, because my mind was set.

Of all the fucked-up shit to hold on to, my mess of a head was holding on to bonding.

Goddamn bonding.

Shaila Victoria Hawkins had been my woman, and I was bonded to her.

For life.

She'd given me everything, right down to her life. I owed her mine, but I couldn't repay a dead woman, so I didn't get another woman to keep. And I sure as fuck didn't deserve to take another woman. I didn't even want to. Four goddamn years and I couldn't stomach the thought of my cock in any other cunt.

Which was a fucking problem, because before I drew my next breath, Decima dropped to her knees and focused her gaze on my junk.

"Decima," I clipped, short and lethal. "Get the fuck up."

She didn't move. She looked at my growing hard-on. "You need to release."

Jesus fucking Christ, she was bold for a compound woman. In fact, too bold. A thought occurred to me that I hadn't considered before. "Were you bonded?"

Heat hit her cheeks, and she dropped her gaze.

"Answer me," I barked.

She flinched, and words flew out of her mouth. "Hero invoked his one passage against the holy one when he came to take me after my first monthlies. He protected me from him, and I bedded down with him in his quarters every night after, but he never made me with child."

Jesus. "He didn't get you pregnant on purpose?" That was against compound rules.

"I…" Her voice dropped to a whisper. "I believe so."

What kind of fucked-up shit was that about? "Hero the Hunter?"

She nodded. "Yes."

I remembered him. Huge, silent, and cunning. "So he never fucked you?"

Her head dropped lower, right along with her voice. "He did. He just never… completed inside me."

"Why?"

"I do not know."

"You fertile?"

Her hands twisted. "Yes."

"He gay?" I'd met plenty of gay dudes in the Army, but never any on the compound. At least none that were open about it.

Confused, she looked up at me. "What?"

"Did he like to fuck men?" I clarified.

Her chest rose and fell once. "He seemed to like taking me."

I snorted. Of course he did. Decima had big tits for a compound woman. "Get up."

"But I—"

"I said get up. I'm done talking about Hero. I don't give a shit what he did or didn't do."

She got up, but she didn't lift her head.

I tipped her chin. "Listen carefully, because this is the last time I'm gonna say this." I waited a beat. "I'm not fucking you. You're not fucking me. You don't owe me sex or anything else. You're not in River Ranch anymore, and the world doesn't work like that. You don't owe any man a fucking thing. Not from here on out. You are your own woman. You make your own rules. Understand?"

Her hazel eyes studying me didn't waver. "No."

"You will. You're gonna take the time after I go back to get your head straight. Morrison will be here next week to help you get your driver's license, then you'll have more freedom. Go to the store, go shopping, walk the beach, fuck, watch TV all day if you want. I don't give a shit. Just take care of the house and keep your head down. Decima is dead, and you don't want anyone to know you're River Ranch. You hear me? *No one.* If you do, you're dead. Understand?"

If he didn't already, River Stephens would have a price on her head. It's what he did with all members who escaped River Ranch with their lives intact.

"I understand."

"Good." I released her. "Be strong and look out for yourself. No one else in this world will."

"You have looked out for me," she quietly corrected.

After four years of simmering anger and a straight diet of killing, all in the name of protecting the United States of America, you'd think the next words that came out of my mouth would be easy as shit to say because I no longer had a conscience.

But they weren't.

"Don't mistake my actions for caring or any kind of loyalty to you because we share a past." She needed to understand she'd never get more out of me than she already had. "You're on your own now." Just like I was.

The words hit her hard, but she tried to hide it. Inhaling, she kept her eyes from welling, but then she said the last thing I was expecting. "I am sorry for enticing you to give me a flower."

Four years of pent-up rage and grief, Ranger training meant to break you, deployments and countless fucking combat missions, and I'd never snapped. I'd never lost my fucking shit. Not since the night my woman and unborn child died.

But all of a sudden, five feet four inches of my past was staring me in the face, apologizing for shit I did, and I couldn't fucking breathe.

I didn't snap. I got enraged.

Irrationally fucking *enraged*.

"*I'm*. NOT *I am*," I viciously bit out. "Listen and learn how the fuck people speak outside the compound. They use contractions. They use slang. They swear. Fucking blend in." Hating her for being alive when my woman wasn't, I shoved past her. "Be ready in two minutes. We're going to the grocery store, and you're driving the goddamn car home."

I stormed down the hall to the master bedroom and slammed the door shut behind me.

Then I drove my fist into the wall three fucking times.

With my knuckles bleeding, I dropped to my goddamn knees and let a name pass my lips that I never spoke aloud anymore.

"Goddamn it, Shaila," my hoarse voice rasped. "*I fucking miss you.*"

Chapter Five

Candle

WARY OF ME, KEEPING HER DISTANCE, DECIMA—*FUCK*—Kendall, pushed the grocery cart down the aisle. Picking shit off the shelves, looking at them, then putting them back, she kept to items I'd seen stocked at the compound.

When she picked up yet another thing and put it back after looking at the box, I snapped. "You have to learn how to read. Tell Morrison to help you with that."

"I know how to read," she quietly replied.

"Since when?" It wasn't a question. It was an accusation.

She didn't fucking notice. "Since I was seven turns or so."

"Years," I corrected. "Not turns."

Unfazed, she picked up the next thing and put it back.

"Hurry it up." I didn't give a shit what she picked out, I just needed her to move it along. After my fucking breakdown in the bedroom, I was done being here. I'd called and booked my flights back. "I'm leaving this afternoon."

She stopped pushing the cart and looked up at me like a wounded animal. "I thought you had a few more days."

"You thought wrong."

"The agent said—"

"Morrison isn't my commanding officer. I need to get back to my squad." I grabbed a box of random shit and threw it in the cart because a small part of me felt guilty for being an asshole to her. "You'll be fine. I'm leaving you with money and the car you picked out." Fucking cage. She'd gone for the cheapest, boxiest piece of shit on the used car lot yesterday, and I'd bought it just to get the hell out of there. "You have Morrison's number. Call him if you need anything while I'm gone."

After a beat, she nodded, then casually picked a box off the shelf and pretended to read the ingredients. "When will you be back?"

"Never if I get fucking killed downrange."

With a shaking hand, she put the box back on the shelf, but she didn't say shit.

Inhaling, I tried to rein it in. "Eleven months," I corrected. I'd have five years in by then, and I could get out. As long as I had my guns lined up, I'd make the move. Buying the cases of Israeli Tavors wasn't the problem. Getting them to the States without getting fucking caught and tried for treason? Near impossible.

But I was working on it.

Which was why I needed to get the fuck back.

Pushing the cart with purpose now, Decima-turned-Kendall nodded. "I'm almost done."

Purposely not commenting on her contraction, I follow

her as she threw more items in the cart and pushed it toward the checkout.

When I was downrange, I thought about my woman. I thought about her every fucking forsaken day. But I was also neck deep in hunting and killing high-value targets and covertly trying to find a way to get crates of guns shipped stateside. If I didn't have my rifle in my hands, I was eating or sleeping, which kept my head in check.

But being back in Florida, every single memory of her was magnified.

Every step, every fucking breath I took, I thought of her. I should've been coming back for her. It should've been me and her buying a goddamn beach house. She should've been here waiting for me, holding our kid as I got off that plane.

Instead I was looking at a woman with the wrong hair color, wrong color eyes, and entirely wrong attitude toward life. Not to mention, my woman would've been jealous as fuck seeing a River Ranch chick get dumped in my lap.

Kendall pushed the cart down the next aisle and paused in front of the period shit.

She glanced at me.

"Don't look at me for that kinda stuff," I warned. "This isn't the compound. You're on your own."

Nodding, she grabbed two boxes and tossed them in the cart.

Irrationally, I hated her for it. I hated her for being here when my woman wasn't, and I knew it was fucked-up to even think that shit when I could empathize with exactly what kind of culture shock she was going through, but goddamn, I wasn't going to pretend I was anything other than what I was. I wasn't righteous, and I sure as fuck wasn't anyone's hero.

Kendall bent down to look at something on a lower shelf, and her long hair fell over her shoulder. Hair that wasn't strawberry blonde.

I grabbed a box of the darkest hair dye I saw and threw it in the cart. "Dye your hair when you get home and cut it shorter. It'll make you less recognizable."

Compound submissive, she didn't argue. "Okay."

I couldn't help but think how my woman would've lit into me if I'd told her to dye her hair black. She also would've given me shit for a day over it, busting my balls and telling me to fuck off without ever cursing.

Goddamn, I needed out of my memories and out of here.

My chest was growing tighter by the second. Worse, the fuel of rage I used to live and breathe wasn't driving me as I stood in a damn grocery store on domestic soil. I wasn't thinking about revenge. I wasn't visualizing my knife stabbing into Hawkins's chest or firing my gun point-blank against Stephens's temple. I wasn't even thinking about the fifty fucking hurdles I needed to jump over to get goddamn Tavors into the country without being caught.

I just fucking missed her.

I missed my woman.

And I was a pussy for even thinking it, but I'd trade killing Stone and River to get her back, if even for one day. In a fucking heartbeat, I would trade all the rage and hate and plans of revenge.

Just to hold her.

Just to see her smile. Hear her voice. Smell her hair. Feel her in my arms.

Goddamn it, Shaila, why'd you let your piece of shit junkie mother get to you, *why?*

"Tarquin?"

Mentally shaking my head, I threw Kendall a warning look. "Candle. That's my name now. Use it."

She stopped pushing the cart and looked up at me in confusion. "Candle? That is your first name?"

"Yeah." Fuck. I knew what she was going to ask before the next sentence left her mouth.

"Why are named after an object?"

I glared at her.

Immediately dropping eye contact and her head, she focused on the cart. "Sorry."

"Don't apologize. Remember what the hell to call me."

"Of course." She pushed the cart down the last aisle, and my woman's voice filtered into my head.

Light a candle for our baby. Save his little soul. Make sure he goes to heaven. Light a candle.

"I'm all done," Kendall quietly said.

Lost in my past, wearing fatigues because I didn't have any normal clothes, I led Kendall to the checkout and swiped my card.

The jailbait cashier smiled shyly at me. "Thank you for your service."

Uncomfortable as hell every time I heard that, I tipped my chin, but I didn't say dick.

Kendall was silent until we got to the car. "Why do people say that to you?"

"Freedom isn't free." Neither was I, but I wasn't going to burden her with Hawkins's blackmail hold over me, my plan, or the hundred things that could go wrong. With any luck, I'd make it home in one piece, get to River and Hawkins, and disappear into the Glades before anyone was the wiser.

But in case I didn't, in case something happened to me, I'd given Kendall the log in for the bank account Morrison had set up in my name. I told her to drain it if something happened to me.

"I don't think anything is free," Kendall mused, pulling me out of my thoughts.

Not bothering to comment, I threw the bags in the trunk. "Get behind the wheel. You're driving home."

Walking to the driver side, she got behind the wheel. Starting the car like she'd driven a hundred times before, she carefully backed out of the space and pulled out of the parking lot. She didn't drive like my woman had, with confidence and joy, but Kendall followed all the directions I'd given her on driving two days ago and managed it fine.

If I was in a charitable mood, I'd tell her she was doing well. In fact, I couldn't think of a single woman from River Ranch who'd handle driving a week off the compound, but I didn't give her any encouragement. If she was going to survive in this world, she'd need to figure out quick how to rely on herself.

A few minutes later, she pulled into the driveway and parked, but before she cut the engine, she turned to me. "Are you angry with me?"

"No." I opened my door.

She reached for my arm. "Candle?"

My muscles stiffened, and I shrugged her off. "What?"

She dropped her hand. "How did you survive?" Her voice lowered. "I heard what they did to you. How did you make it out of the swamp?"

I told her the truth. "I crawled."

For two heartbeats, she stared at me.

Then she surprised me.

She didn't show shock. She didn't show empathy. She didn't show fear. She didn't show any emotion at all. She nodded.

I respected her for it. "Anything else?"

"No."

Tipping my chin, I got out of the car and headed to the trunk to grab the groceries. Kendall joined me, and after we had all the bags, I reached around her to close the trunk.

It happened so fast, I didn't know what the fuck was going on.

Letting out a sound like a wounded animal, she dropped the bags, fell to the ground, and her hands went over her head.

Acting on instinct, my hand went to where a weapon was usually, and I scanned the empty driveway looking for the threat. No weapon, no threat, adrenaline pumping through my veins, I looked down at a cowering woman.

As fast as she'd dropped to the ground, the animosity for her I'd been harboring flipped to guilt.

I crouched. "Kendall."

Her body shaking, her hands over her head, her arm all fucked up with scabbed knife wounds, she didn't respond.

I risked putting my hand between her shoulders. "Decima."

"Please don't..." Her voice shaking, she tried again. "Please don't come up behind me."

Jesus fuck. "River come up behind you?" I knew the fucker had cut her arm.

Still shaking, she didn't answer.

I didn't do comfort. Or reassurance, or any other soft bullshit platitude. I'd hugged exactly twice in my life, and both times were with my woman. I didn't want to fucking hug Decima Stephens. I wanted to kill River though. Except I didn't have a gun and I wasn't on the compound.

So I sat my ass down and pulled a traumatized woman onto my lap. "You're okay." I didn't know what the hell she was. "You're not on the compound anymore. Breathe it out. You're stronger than this. Come on, just breathe." Maybe those weren't the right words, but it was all I had.

For a long moment, she sat stiff as hell. Then slowly her muscles released their tense hold and she relaxed into my arms.

I closed my eyes and longed for something I'd never have again.

"Tarquin?" Her voice small, she shifted on my lap.

I inhaled deep. "I'm not Tarquin anymore, babe. You gotta remember that."

"That's going to take some getting used to," she admitted.

Everything for her would take some getting used to. "Yeah, well, you got about an hour to figure it out before I have to leave."

Her body stiffened again. "I am sorry I reacted the way I did."

"Don't be. There's not a single brother or sister who doesn't carry some kind of scar from that place."

"What is yours?"

I snorted. "You're asking that like you think it's only one. Come on, get up. Let's get this shit inside, and I'll help put it away before I leave."

"Okay." Compound fed, no weight on her, she easily stood.

All of a sudden, I was staring down a memory of my woman after we'd been out in the woods for two months. Her arms were thinner, her thighs were no longer soft, her hip bones were sticking out even though she was pregnant, and her face was just like Decima's was right now. Gaunt.

I remembered my woman telling me she wanted a bag of potato chips.

I never got her the fucking chips.

I could've walked to the gas station she used to work at, bought the damn things and brought them to her.

But I hadn't.

Instead I'd fucked her hard every morning and every night and spent the rest of the time conditioning myself and not giving a shit that as I was putting on muscle weight, she was losing pounds she couldn't afford.

I didn't take care of my woman.

I didn't protect her.

"Candle?"

I blinked. Then I quickly grabbed the bags and made a fucking promise to the universe. "Do me a favor while I'm gone?"

Kendall frowned but agreed. "All right."

I made a vow then and there. "Eat enough while I'm gone. Take care of yourself. If you need something, call Morrison. If he can't help you, tell him to get in touch with me. Understand?" I wouldn't let anything happen to her. I wouldn't let her die because I was negligent.

Kendall nodded. "I understand."

"Good." I walked into the house.

Chapter Six

Candle

I DROPPED MY RUCKSACK ON THE FLOOR BY THE FRONT DOOR. Kendall sat on the couch watching my every move but not making eye contact. She looked small as fuck, and I couldn't help but think if shit were different, I'd be leaving my woman to deploy. The thought making me fucking sick, it was a scenario I hadn't even considered four years ago.

So intent on getting in the military and becoming a Ranger, I saw little else besides the need for a roof overhead that wouldn't blow away in hurricane winds, and a restock of our food supplies before we ran out.

Looking at the woman on my couch, I realized how much had changed in four years.

Naked without a gun, my hands went to my hips. "You're gonna be fine."

"I am not worried about that."

I didn't want to ask what she was worried about, let alone get in a philosophical discussion when the taxi was going to be here in five minutes, but what choice did I have if I didn't want to be a complete dick? "Then what's wrong?"

She dropped her gaze to her lap. "I never belonged at River Ranch."

No shit. "Who did?" River Stephens needed to be put down like a rabid dog.

"Some of the brothers and sisters. Maybe most." She looked back up. "I am worried about you coming back."

There was no hiding the truth of the situation. "I can't control those haji fucks with roadside bombs any more than I can control the weather."

"You are not afraid of dying."

She didn't ask it like a question, but I answered it anyway. "Not anymore." What the fuck did I have to live for besides revenge?

"But once you were?"

I hesitated. "Yes."

"What changed?"

I wasn't telling her about Shaila. The hard sins of my past were mine alone, and my woman's memory belonged to me. "Life happened."

She nodded as if she understood. "I do not fear death either."

"Because?" I shouldn't have bothered asking. We were all taught to embrace death in the name of River Stephens on the compound. Of course she wasn't afraid to die. The only question was if she was brainwashed about it or resigned.

Still, like a lot of women on the compound, she didn't shrug or fidget. But unlike most women from River Ranch, she made eye contact. "I will die one day. When is not up to me, especially if River puts a reward out for my head."

I didn't think she was fucking pining to get back onto the compound. She hadn't once mentioned wanting to be back there, but it was a relief to hear she wasn't blind to the practical reality of her situation either.

She knew as well as I did how River operated. He made no qualms about telling every victim on that compound what would happen to them if they went against *God's plan* and forsook him.

Not bothering to sugarcoat a damn thing, I didn't bullshit her. "All deserters have a bounty. It's what he does." Sitting in the chair across from her, I leaned my arms on my knees. "But that doesn't necessarily mean anything will happen to you. No one leaves the compound to go actively looking for former members, and River himself sure as fuck never leaves his domain. So as long as you keep your identity secret, you're safe."

"I understand."

"Good." I made to get up.

A short flash of surprise crossed her expression, but she said nothing.

"What?" I demanded.

"You do care if I live or die."

Christ. I sat back down. "You want the fucking truth?"

She didn't hesitate. "Yes."

"I don't want your death on my hands, but that's as far as this goes. I'm no one's hero, and I'm not your savior." I wasn't going to pretend I had any familial loyalty to her. I wasn't bonded to her, I wasn't fucking her, and I sure as hell wasn't going to hold her hand. I only planned on making sure she didn't die because of something I neglected to do. She was here, and she was safe for now, and that's where my responsibility ended.

No shock or surprise in her expression this time, she held my gaze. "I was not expecting… friendship."

Fucking hell. "I don't even know what that word means, woman." Yeah, I served alongside men I would die for, but that didn't mean we sat around off mission shooting the shit. More than a drink or two, I didn't spend time with anyone I didn't have to, including my LT or any of the soldiers I served with.

She nodded like a damn thing about either one of us or this conversation was normal. "All right. So I lay my head here until you come home. Then you bed here too, but separately."

This time I didn't bother correcting her compound speak. "Yes."

"Then what?"

The taxi pulled up and honked.

"You live, Decima. You fucking live." I stood and grabbed my rucksack.

She rose to her feet, and I heard it.

Pipes.

Lots of fucking pipes.

Motherfucker.

I spared Decima a warning look. "Get in your room and lock the door. Do not come out until you hear the motorcycles leave, no matter what. If you hear shots fired, call Morrison and tell him the Lone Coasters are here." *Goddamn it*, why didn't I tell Morrison to get me a fucking gun?

"Who are the Lone Coasters?"

"Bikers, woman, *bikers*. The shit I warned you about the other day. I hope like fuck you were listening, because I sure as hell wasn't talking just to hear myself talk."

"I remember, you just did not speak the name Lone Coasters."

I didn't have time for this. "Go to the bedroom, *now*."

I waited until she hurried down the hall and locked herself in her room. Then I shouldered my rucksack and opened the front door as a dozen bikers pulled in behind the taxi.

Front and center was Stone fucking Hawkins.

Cutting his engine, he pushed his sunglasses up, and a sick grin spread across his face. "Long time, Scott."

I shut the front door behind me. "Not long enough. What the fuck do you want? I've got a plane to catch."

Fucker nodded like he knew my plans. "I heard."

I called his bluff. "You didn't hear shit."

"You sure? Because you're going back downrange for the last time before you get out and come work for me. Very patriotic of you."

Asshole. He was lucky I wasn't armed. I would've killed him on the spot. "You that desperate, you counting my time in the service now?"

He laughed like he had the upper hand. "No, not desperate at all, son. How is Afghanistan by the way? You get any good opium? I hear there're lots of poppy fields."

I put zero stock in his Afghanistan question. Every news station was talking about the action there. He didn't know where the fuck I was deployed to, and I didn't give a shit about his posturing. But for the first time in four years,

I did question why the hell he hadn't killed me the night my woman died. Trying to blackmail me into working for him after I served my time in the Army was a fool's mission. He had to know I'd try to kill him.

"I know what you're thinking." Hawkins smirked. "But you're not going to kill me."

"You sure about that?"

He smiled. "Oh, yeah."

I scanned the fucking bikers. Two I recognized from that night four years ago. Four more looked like the fucks who'd ridden off scared, leaving their dead brothers behind at his property. All of them were useless. Any one of the Rangers I served with would wipe the fucking floor with their asses. "Keep thinking that, asshole."

Hawkins chuckled. "I will."

I walked to the taxi, opened the back door and threw my rucksack in. Pausing, I turned to Hawkins. "You know what your critical mistake was?"

Faking a frown, the fucker crossed his arms and tilted his head like he was thinking. "Can't say I recall making any critical mistakes."

I laid it out. "You neglected to take into consideration one very important fact."

He scratched his beard. "Did I?"

"I don't give a single fuck about my life. Take your blackmail bullshit and loser bikers and get the fuck outta here. The day I come work for you is the day hell freezes over." I got in the taxi.

Stone strode to the passenger side and motioned at the driver to put my window down.

Looking like he was going to piss himself, the driver couldn't open my window fast enough as he muttered a bullshit apology. "Sorry."

Stone played off his mild expression like the psychopath he was. "Then I guess hell is about to freeze over, *brother*." Leaning down, he dropped his voice and his smile. "As long as you show back up in eleven months and do what the fuck you're told, your little hazel-eyed secret inside will be untouched. But if you don't, I'll hand her over to the club. When they're done gangbanging her, I'll make sure she's tortured nice and slow." He paused for effect. "She'll be begging for death." Abruptly standing back up, he slapped the hood of the taxi. "Better get a move on, driver. This Ranger has a plane to catch."

The taxi driver, frozen in his seat, didn't move.

"Drive," Stone barked as the bikers behind us pulled out of our way.

Flinching, the driver threw the car in reverse.

Stone grinned. "See you in eleven months, *Sergeant*."

The driver burned rubber backing out into the street before he spun the wheel and threw it in drive.

"Wait," I ordered. "Don't fucking drive off yet." I wasn't leaving until they did.

Practically shaking with fear, the driver glanced in the rearview mirror at me. "That's Stone Hawkins. I think we should do what he says."

"I know who the hell it is, and I'm paying for this ride, so fucking wait."

His hands shaking on the wheel, the driver nodded.

One by one, I watched those biker fucks take off. Then Hawkins rolled his Hog up to my window.

I glared at him. "You do know I'm going to kill you, right?"

He laughed. "Maybe. Or maybe you'll enjoy working for me." He winked. "It'll be a lot like you're used to in the Rangers, except much more lucrative. You'll get to whip my boys into shape. Teach them to shoot." He leaned forward and lowered his voice conspiratorially. "Teach them to be killers like you." He leaned back up and saluted me. "Stay strong, soldier." Revving his Harley, he took off.

"Airport," I clipped at the driver, pulling out the phone my lieutenant had given me.

Two rings, and Decima picked up the cell I'd bought her a couple days ago. "Hello?" she whispered.

"You're safe for now." Hawkins was a lot of things, but the asshole had a hard-on for me. He wouldn't fuck with Kendall and risk his leverage before he got what he wanted out of me. "But don't go near any Lone Coaster fucks. You see a biker, *any* biker, stay away like I told you. Understand?"

"I understand."

"I'll see you in eleven months." Whether I was ready or not, I was getting out of the Rangers.

Chapter Seven

Shaila

My lips chapped, my eyes crusted from sleep, from tears, I gingerly rolled toward the nightstand. My limbs aching, my head pounding, my pussy sore, I hurt everywhere. I was so thirsty, I could've committed murder for a glass of water. And I would have, heaven be damned, if I could've lifted an arm and yielded a knife with enough force to kill.

But I couldn't.

I only had one goal in my sights.

Two actually.

Two, small, round white goals.

Ignoring the naked, snoring, sweat-soaked, passed-out asshole next to me, I reached for salvation on the nightstand.

My shaking fingers covered the two pills, and I slid them onto my palm so I didn't drop them on the floor. My legs wouldn't hold me in a damn crawl right now if you held a gun to my head.

The pills securely in my hand, I fell to my back and

brought them to my mouth. Ignoring the glass of water that'd been right next to my fix, I swallowed the painkillers with what little saliva I had left in my mouth.

My throat burning, the acidic taste of manufactured narcotics coated my tongue, but I didn't care.

I lay there.

Waiting.

Willing.

Praying the drugs would melt into my system and take me away from my own damn thoughts sooner rather than later.

The snoring asshole snorted and shifted.

A waft of his body stench hit me and bile rose. Panic had my hand slamming over my mouth, and faster than I thought I was capable of moving, I plugged my nose, held my mouth and sat up.

I will not vomit.

I will not vomit.

I will not vomit.

I wouldn't get any more pills until tonight. That's how it worked. If I threw these up, I would be in for a day of hell I didn't want to think about.

Furiously swallowing down the spit pooling in my mouth, I made to get up and away from the stench in the bed.

"Hey," a smoke-scratchy voice barked. "Where the fuck do you think you're going, whore?"

I took my hand away from my mouth for only a second. "Bathroom. I'm gonna be sick." I stood on unsteady legs.

Grunting assent, he stroked his nasty dick. "Hurry the

fuck back here. You're sucking me off, bitch."

I stumbled toward the filthy bathroom and shut the door behind me. Bracing my hands on the counter, I looked at the bottle of tequila I must've left in here last night. Then did something I usually avoided at all cost.

I looked in the mirror.

Dull hair, sunken eyes, protruding cheekbones, bruises on my neck.

I couldn't help it.

My eyes welled, and I thought of him.

Strong, beautiful, stoic *him*.

Four years.

"Get the fuck back here, whore!"

Four fucking years.

"Junkie whore," I corrected, whispering at the mirror before turning around and raising my voice. "Comin'!" Grabbing the bottle, I threw back... one swallow, two, three.

"Hurry up!" the biker hollered.

Slamming the bottle down, sucking in air through my teeth, I stumbled back into the bedroom.

Chapter

EIGHT

Candle
Three Years Later
Ormond Beach, FL

FUCKING PAROLED.

Six months in jail for assault because the Feds had to charge me with something. The crates of guns I'd worked years to get stateside were fucking gone, Stone Hawkins was in the wind after trying to steal my guns and pissing off the cartel, and River Stephens was still alive.

Fuck my life.

I texted Kendall.

Coming home, baby. Need to see you. Wait for me.

She wasn't going to like what I had to say, but it was time. She needed to find her own damn place to live. I'd fucked her life up enough already. Working for Stone Hawkins as his sergeant-at-arms for two and a half years was the least of it. Never mind the fact I spent that time either killing off members behind Hawkins's back or planting the seed of dissension. My best asset I'd recruited to my side was Stripe. Young and eager, he had a hard-on for the armed forces, and he saw me as a fucking hero.

I texted him after I texted Kendall.

I'm out. Get whoever the fuck is still around and wait for me at the clubhouse. I'm heading home first to handle some business, then I'll meet you there.

My previous plan had been shit, and I was done playing games. I was going to get Kendall out of the way, then go after Hawkins and Stephens. Stripe would round up whoever was around, and those fucks were either in or out. I didn't trust a single one of them, but like Hawkins, I was going to use them for the single fact that it'd be a body holding a gun. Numbers were numbers, and I needed a goddamn army to ride up to the gates at River Ranch.

After getting processed out and putting on my own clothes, I took a cab home. My intent was to tell Kendall she was moving out, have a damn drink, then go to the clubhouse and rally a bunch of bikers I hated.

Riding into the Glades with weapons drawn wasn't a bright fucking plan, but it was *the* plan now. I was going to kill River Stephens if I had to walk over the dead bodies of compound brothers and sisters to get a clean shot.

Once River drew his last breath, I was going to find Stone and make him bleed.

Then, maybe I'd be able to fucking breathe again.

If not, I'd still ride into the Glades and never come out.

The cab pulled up to my house, and I cursed. Next to the piece-of-shit Jetta Kendall had picked out on the used car lot three years ago, an SUV I didn't recognize was parked in my driveway.

I tossed money at the cab driver. "Keep the change."

The second I opened the car door, I heard yelling coming from inside the house. Pissed, I stalked up my driveway. No weapon on me, my only advantage surprise, I threw open my front door.

Un-fucking-believable.

André Luna. Pretty boy security expert. Holding Kendall from behind like a fucking amateur.

Instead of looking like a Marine who owned the tightest personal security firm in the business, his face was pinched, his stance was defensive, and he had a gash on the side of his head that was dripping blood all over my fucking floor.

"Put her down, Luna." I was pissed that he was here, but I also saw opportunity. We'd crossed paths over the years, and while I hated the fucker, I couldn't deny he was solid. He could take Kendall with him.

"Stand the fuck down, Scott," Luna barked.

"I hate you!" Kendall screamed, flailing against Luna's hold.

Christ, not even seven in the morning, and she was drunk. "Don't grab her from behind." I glared at Luna, but then I took Kendall's face in both of my hands and forced an even tone. "Take a fucking breath, baby. Right now." She still panicked when anyone came up behind her.

"*I hate you!*" Reeking of alcohol, she kicked me in the thigh.

"No, you don't." But she should.

"You left me!" she yelled.

An ounce of guilt hit, but I shoved it down. I didn't have time for this shit. "Who takes care of you?" I demanded.

"You *left me*." She went slack, but Luna didn't let go of her, which said a whole damn lot.

"I didn't leave," I corrected. "I got locked up."

In a move she never would've done sober, she wrapped her arms around my neck and threw down her own brand of accusation. "You left me alone."

Half out of guilt, half to stick it to Luna, I picked her up and sank to the couch. That FBI agent Morrison had cast her fate by calling me three years ago, but I'd sealed it by bringing her here. Being connected to me was a shit prospect for anyone. I owed her at least a few minutes of my time. "I know, but I'm here now."

Giving me a look of disgust, Luna turned toward the front door at the exact moment the sound of custom pipes filled my small-ass living room.

"Luna, wait. I need to talk to you." Stripe, that fucker. I was going to throttle him for coming to my damn house.

Luna reached for the door. "Not happening."

"This isn't about me," I amended.

The prick turned around like he was doing me a favor and raised an eyebrow as blood dripped down his face. I didn't ask what happened. I didn't have to. A drinking Kendall wasn't someone you fucked with, and he'd clearly fucked with her.

I nodded toward the hall as Kendall clung to me, which only solidified the fact she'd been on a bender. "First aid kit's in the bathroom." She never would've done this shit sober.

Glaring at me like he wanted to kill me, Luna shook his head. "I'm out." He reached the door, but it burst open.

Five fucking LCs—Link, Deacon, Joey, Stripe and Rip— all walked in.

"Can-daaaaaaal!" Link shouted.

Deacon glanced at Luna and smirked. "Already fucking shit up, Candle?"

Stripe eyed the broken glass on the rug, then put his hand on a holstered 9mm. "Need me to take out the trash?"

Joey eyed Kendall's ass as he grabbed his dick. "Fuck yeah, let's team this bitch." He lifted the hem of her nightshirt.

Luna pulled his piece and aimed at him. "Hands off."

I smacked Joey's hand. "You so much as fucking breathe on her and you're dead." I glared at every asshole LC. "She's under my protection."

Stripe stood stone-faced while Link, Deacon, and Joey all looked at me like they hadn't heard this exact same warning a thousand times before.

But Rip didn't even glance at me.

The asshole drew and aimed at Kendall's head. His psychotic fucking glare cut from her back to me. "*What the fuck? Are you fucking kidding me, Sarge?*"

For a split second I was thrown.

Then it hit me.

When Joey had lifted Kendall's shirt, Rip saw it. He saw the goddamn branding on her back that was the exact same as mine. Two Rs, back to back. River Ranch.

Fuck.

Fuck.

Luna trained his aim on Rip.

"Drop it, Rip," I warned. I should've killed him and Link years ago. Those fucking assholes were there the night my woman died. They deserved to die, but I'd stupidly kept them alive because they'd been closest to Hawkins and I'd thought I could use that to my advantage.

"No fucking way," Rip seethed. "Do you know who—"

"Shut the fuck up!" I dumped Kendall off my lap and got in Rip's face. The asshole was so fucking slow I'd grabbed the barrel of his gun and shoved it down before he drew his next breath. "Walk the fuck outside, *now!*"

Like the tool he was, Rip spat at my feet. "This ain't over." He walked out.

Clueless or just plain stupid, Link dropped to the couch next to Kendall.

I glared at Deacon, Joey and Stripe. "I told you all to wait at the clubhouse."

Luna aimed at Link.

Link smirked. "What clubhouse, Sarge?" He fingered the hem of Kendall's short-as-fuck nightshirt.

"Try that again," Luna warned, "and it'll be your last move."

Kendall slapped Link's hand. "Fuck you, small dick. Don't touch me."

I'd had enough. I grabbed Link by the front of his shirt. "Get the fuck out of my house, Link."

The asshole held his hands up as he grinned at me. "Didn't do nothing, Sarge, but I'll wait outside. Keep Rip company."

I shoved him toward the door. "*Out.*" Glaring at the rest of them, I gave the same order. "All of you, get the fuck out. I got business with Luna." Luna needed to get Kendall the hell out of here before Rip started making calls. Because Kendall didn't just have any bounty on her head, she was the fucking jackpot to these assholes.

Deacon chuckled. "We'll give you ten, Sarge. Should be enough time to handle your shit and get your dick wet. Come on, assholes." He walked out with Joey and Stripe following. Except Stripe paused before the door and glanced at me. In a covert sign of solidarity, he tipped his chin.

Luna holstered his piece after the front door closed.

I leveled Kendall with a look. "I told you not to taunt them." Now I was going to have to handle Rip before he opened his fucking mouth and told every LC out there how much Kendall was worth to River Stephens. And a dead Rip wouldn't do shit to help me find out where Hawkins was hiding.

"Hey," Luna barked. "She didn't do a damn thing."

"Stay the fuck outta this," I warned Luna.

His stare cunning, Luna narrowed his eyes. "Who did Rip think she was?"

"I'm right here, and I don't need to listen to you assholes talk about me." Kendall stood up.

Out of patience, I laid into her. "I'm out five goddamn minutes and you're already getting into it? You're not supposed to fucking drink."

"And your asshole bikers aren't supposed to pull a gun on me!"

"Jesus Christ, woman. What the fuck is wrong with you?" She knew how fucking serious this was. And now she'd just made my life a hell of a lot more complicated.

"You heard Cuban Boy," she taunted. "I didn't do anything wrong."

Was she serious? "You were drinking before sunup!"

"They came back!" she yelled.

My jaw ticked, and I tried to rein it in. I knew she had nightmares courtesy of fucking River Stephens, but that should've been more reason to keep her shit together, not day drink or drink all night or whatever the fuck she'd been doing. "We've been through this," I reminded her. She'd been prescribed sleeping pills a year ago. "You know what to do."

"No." She pushed me away. "I'm not taking pills to fucking sleep."

"Goddamn it, woman." Out of time, I gave up arguing with her. "Get some clothes on and pack a bag. You're going with Luna."

"If she's coming with me, I want answers," Luna demanded.

Self-righteous fuck. I barely spared him a glance. "All you need to know is she's going with you."

Alarm spread across Kendall's face. "You promised."

I knew what she meant. I'd promised her she could stay with me. But that was then, and this was now. Done with this conversation, needing to get to Rip to do damage control, I gripped Kendall's chin so she'd know I wasn't fucking around. "You know how this works. I make the rules, you follow them. Get. *Dressed.*"

Spitting words out with a newfound venom, she shoved me. "Fuck you, you worthless piece of shit *biker.*"

I forced a smile just to get her to hurry the fuck up and get moving. "That's my girl. Now go clean up."

She stomped to her bedroom and slammed the door.

I turned on Luna. "What the fuck did you do to set her off? Why's she drinking?" A nightmare didn't usually send her into a tailspin. But having him here might.

Glaring at me, he ignored my question. "You lied."

"I lie about a lot of shit." Walking to the kitchen, I grabbed a towel off the oven door and tossed it at him. "You're gonna have to be more specific."

He grabbed it and pressed it to his head. "Who the hell did Rip think she was?"

"No one," I lied.

"She's your woman." Fucker stated it like he wasn't testing the waters.

I laughed without an ounce of humor. "I thought you were smart, Marine." The prick had it bad for her, which was just as well.

"I know what I saw, *Ranger*." He pulled the towel back and glanced at it. "Sober her up, then tell her she's fired. Talon replaced her when she didn't show up for work all last week." He tossed the towel on the counter and turned to walk out.

Shit. "Wait."

He paused, but he didn't turn around. "What?"

I took the in. "I need a favor."

He turned. "You're not in a position to ask a favor. Find someone else."

I ignored him, because I knew the look on his face. He was jonesing for a reason to take her with him, and I was handing it to him on a silver platter. "I need you to get her out of here. A few days, a week. I'm cleaning up what's left of the LCs. Then I'm regrouping." It was bullshit. I wasn't going to regroup a damn thing. I'd probably kill every fucker that was just in here and anyone else Rip told about Kendall before this was over. Giving him fair warning, I said as much as I could. "It's gonna get bloody."

Luna didn't take the bait. "Find someone else to babysit your girlfriend."

"Goddamn it. She's not my fucking girlfriend." Jesus, he was beating a dead horse. "She never was."

"Who is she?" he demanded.

Christ. "She's my fucking responsibility, okay?"

"You're an asshole," Kendall bit out.

We both turned at the sound of her voice.

Still not dressed, her arms crossed, Kendall stood in the living room glaring her ass off at me. "I never asked you to take care of me."

"Jesus fuck," I muttered. "I'm not having this conversation. You know how it ends. Get some clothes on, woman. You're going with Luna for a few days."

She eyed her keys on the counter, then her gaze cut to the front door.

"*Shit.*" I knew that look from her.

In the next second, she was moving.

"Luna," I barked.

"On it." Closer to her than I was, he reached for her. "Incoming."

"Right behind you." I moved in on his six.

Grabbing her from behind, he tossed her to me like she was a live grenade.

Kendall shrieked. "Put me down!"

Holding her tight as fuck so she didn't kick me, I leveled with her. "You know I don't ask you for anything."

"I hate you," she spat.

"I know." Kicking her out was a shit move, but she'd be glad for it in the long run.

"I don't have all day," Luna interrupted. "I've got a plane waiting."

Ignoring the prick, I spoke to Kendall. "You need to do this for me. You need to go with him."

The fight left her body as her muscles relaxed marginally, but she still gave me lip. "I have to work."

"You lost your job when you didn't show last week. Luna was here to deliver the message." Setting her down, I grabbed her face, then I did something I never fucking did. I asked. "I'm just asking for a few days. Then maybe you can come home." I had no intention of letting her come back here.

She crossed her arms in Kendall attitude, but her tone gave away her Decima insecurities. "This isn't my home."

"I hear you, babe, loud and clear." I did, but we were out of time. "Go get dressed."

For once she fucking did what I said.

Luna leveled me with a look after her door closed. "Start talking."

"Can't." Wasn't my place to tell him. Grabbing the whiskey off the coffee table, I threw back and closed my eyes against the burn I hadn't felt in six months. "You know what you miss most when you're locked up?" I glanced at Luna. "Besides pussy?" Which I hadn't felt in seven long fucking years.

"Freedom," Luna clipped like he knew what the hell it was like to be locked up. "What the fuck just happened?"

"Nothing." I took another long swig, then exhaled through my teeth. "I don't give a shit about freedom." Jail was a cakewalk compared to compound life. "But whiskey?"

I glanced at the bottle. "That, I give a fuck about." It was the closest high I could get to sinking inside my woman, but I'd lost that right when I lost her, and I didn't deserve another shot at happiness, so whiskey it was.

"I can think of another thing you give a fuck about," Luna said dryly.

He didn't know shit. If six months locked up had taught me anything, it was that life was short and I'd wasted years not pulling the trigger. Murder was now the only fucking thing I cared about.

I nodded toward the hall. "Yeah. Well, that just makes me stupid." I never should've let Hawkins hold her over my head.

Luna tried to play hardball. "Answer my question, or I'm not doing you any favors."

I chuckled. "You'll take her. I see the way you look at her." I used to look at my woman that way—alpha, dominant and possessive as fuck.

"Which time? When I was wondering why the hell she was drinking at six a.m., or when she was trying to headbutt me after catching her before she pitched face-first into the coffee table?"

I put the bottle down, but I wanted to drink the whole damn thing. "Don't grab her from behind, and you'll be fine." I turned toward the front door. "I got shit to handle. Good luck with her." He was going to fucking need it. More than he'd ever know.

"All right. I'll take her on one condition."

"You think you're owed a condition?" No one was owed anything in this life.

"You don't have another option," he challenged.

"You're in my fucking house, without permission, and you're still breathing. That's your fucking *condition*." Motherfucker.

"Fine. She stays."

I could smell his bullshit. "Why are you even here?"

"Same reason you gave her. Talerco sent me."

"Right. Keep lying to yourself. Like that won't catch up to you." Fucker better watch his shit.

"You really wanna go down that road, pendejo?" Luna nodded toward the front door. "You're the one with his past sitting outside waiting to fucking pounce on your woman."

He still couldn't let it go. Fucking idiot. "My past ain't got nothing on hers."

"What's she coming from?"

"Nothing," I lied. "Get her out of here."

"I'm not taking her against her will."

I didn't care if he dragged her out by her hair at this point. She was dead if she stayed here. "Take her to your place, and when she sobers up, I'll talk to her. She knows I have club business to handle. She'll know it's better for her to not be around."

"What club business?"

"Damage control." If I wasn't too late after wasting my time talking to him. Otherwise, I'd be digging graves.

"What's left to control?"

"My reputation." I walked out the door.

Chapter Nine

Candle

THE SECOND I STEPPED OUTSIDE, RIP WAS IN MY FACE.
"Do you know who the fuck that is?" Agitated, reeking of booze and sweat, his eyes were dilated.

Stepping around him, itching to get to my bike, I opened my garage and tried to play it off. "Whoever you think she is, you're fucking wrong." I straddled my bike and fired it up. The engine purred to life like I'd driven it yesterday, and all I wanted to do was ride, but I had to deal with fucking Rip first.

"I'm not fucking wrong," he yelled over the pipes.

Backing the bike out, I cut the engine, threw the kickstand and reluctantly got off. After closing the garage door, I tipped my chin toward the others who were huddled together like it'd protect them from my wrath. "What'd you tell them?"

"You think I'm stupid? What the fuck do you think I told them? We're gonna be rich, asshole. So step the fuck aside. I'm going after a two-million-dollar bounty." His gun in his hand, he shoved at my chest.

"You make me fucking shoot you, Rip, I won't miss."

Stepping back, the asshole drew, then Link, Deacon and Joey followed suit.

"You're outnumbered," Rip warned. "Give us the River Ranch bitch. You been hiding her long enough."

"Deacon, Joey, you with this asshole?" My eyes on Rip, I threw the question over my shoulder but I didn't bother asking Link because I knew where his loyalties was. "You both want to die too?"

"Hand the bitch over, Sarge," Link ground out. "Or you're gonna be the one to die."

I didn't hesitate.

Grabbing Rip's gun, I elbowed the fucker in the face, spun and shot Link between the eyes. Then I gave Deacon and Joey one warning. "Get the fuck out of here and keep your mouths shut or I will hunt you both down and gut you."

Joey and Deacon held their aim until Stripe spoke up. "Come on. Let's get out of here before a neighbor calls the cops." Shoving his piece in his back waistband, he walked to his bike, but just like inside, he glanced back at me and tipped his chin before they all got on their bikes and took off.

As I watched them leave, I caught movement out of the corner of my eye, and glanced at Rip. The fucker was pulling a piece out of an ankle holster.

"Draw and you're dead," I warned.

The idiot not only drew, he fired.

His aim shit, his single shot hit me in the shoulder.

I double tapped. Two in the chest so the asshole would feel himself dying.

The impact throwing him back, he hit my front door, bursting it open. Nothing to break his fall, he landed on his back half in, half out of my house as his gun skittered across my floor.

My shoulder on fire, I stepped over him, kicked his legs free of the path of the door, then slammed it shut.

"How many more?" Luna demanded as he glanced out the window with his gun drawn.

"It's handled." I aimed at Rip's head.

"There were four shots. Two are in the asshole on the floor, and you're hit. That leaves one shot and three bikes in the driveway." Luna ticked off stats like I gave a fuck.

"I said, it's *handled*." I kicked Rip in the leg. "Get the fuck up." Pain radiating from my shoulder, blood rapidly spreading across my shirt, I wanted to fucking shoot him again.

Rip groaned.

Luna scanned the front yard. "Where's the second LC?"

"Dead." Like they all should've been. "Next to the front hedge. Drag him inside or get Kendall the fuck outta here."

Rip lifted a shaking hand and pointed toward the kitchen. "She's fucking dead," he sputtered, coughing up blood. "She's not gonna bring us down."

I jammed his own damn 9mm against his forehead. "What the fuck are you gonna do? You're bleeding out faster than you can crawl to your gun."

"Dead," Rip spat the word out. "LCs first." He wheezed. "Shoot the Riv—"

I pulled the trigger.

The back of Rip's head exploded, and Kendall screamed. "Candle!"

"Goddamn it," I growled at Luna. "Get her *the fuck* outta here."

Finally getting the message, Luna moved. "Come on, chica, we're going."

Kendall stared at what was left of Rip. "He was going to kill me?"

"Luna," I warned.

The motherfucker closed his fist and held it up, giving me the hold signal as he spoke to her. "You need me to pack you a bag, chica?"

Kendall's gaze cut from the body to me. "He knew?"

Shoving the gun in my back waistband, compartmentalizing the pain, I yanked my T-shirt off and pressed it to my shoulder. Then I leveled Kendall with a look. "You got two minutes. Get the fuck outta here or Luna's going to carry you out."

Her face twisted with anger, and she let loose. "You fucking told him? *You goddamn asshole, you told him?*"

I ground my back teeth. "I didn't say shit."

"He fucking knew," she accused.

"Not my fucking fault," I threw it back on her. "Keep your goddamn clothes on next time."

"I'm dressed!"

"Jesus fucking Christ," I roared. "I didn't do shit but look after you." And now I had to do damage control with a goddamn bum shoulder. Through and through or not, it fucking hurt.

She kept fucking going. "By telling him!"

I lost my shit. "I didn't tell him! I didn't fucking say shit, and you know that. Get *the fuck* out of here so I can clean up your goddamn mess!"

"I don't need you," Kendall yelled back. "I can take care of myself!" She skirted a wide berth around the mess on the floor that used to be Rip and fled to her room.

"I swear to fucking God." I kicked over a side table.

Luna glanced out the front window before looking back at me. "What the fuck just happened?"

"Nothing." I nodded toward the driveway. "Her car's too fucking small. That your SUV?"

"Rental."

"You take out the extra insurance?" I needed to get rid of the bodies, and unless I got some help, my only choice was to torch them because I wasn't digging shit with my shoulder now.

Luna knew what I was asking. Thankfully, he tossed his keys at me. "Take it, but my prints are in there. You better fucking wipe it down," he warned.

Snatching the keys out of the air with my bad arm, I winced. "I know what the fuck I'm doing."

"From where I'm standing, it sure as hell doesn't look like it." He glanced down the hall.

"Yeah, it wouldn't. Not to a fucking golden boy like you." I'd wager everything I had he wasn't digging graves by the time he was five.

All business, he didn't touch my insult. "I'm getting her out. But I'm done with your cagey bullshit. Give me something."

For once, I wished I could. It'd make his job a lot easier. But it wasn't my place to tell him. All I could do now was hand the reins over. Kendall deserved that much. "Protect her."

"I can't do my job if you don't tell me—"

"Assume the worst," I interrupted as Kendall came out of her bedroom.

Walking into the living room with a bag over her shoulder, Kendall aimed her best glare at me. "You're dead to me." She stepped around the mess and slammed the door behind her.

Chapter
TEN

Shaila

I HURT. EVERYWHERE.

I always hurt.

The drugs, the alcohol, the bikers using me like I was nothing but a damn hole for them to come in—I didn't even remember why I was still doing this.

"Why?" I yelled out to no one as the beat of shitty music from downstairs in the clubhouse thumped through my room.

My room.

I laughed and took another swig of tequila straight from the bottle, but then the pain came back. At first it was in my shoulder. Then it was all over my body. Nausea hit, and I forced myself to sit up.

My feet on the ground, my head swam.

Pain, fucking tequila, oxy—I knew those feelings. I knew what my body felt after being used and abused, and I hit the bottle after one of the asshole bikers fed me my pills like candy.

But this felt like a different kind of pain.

A no-coming-back-from-it pain.

Maybe that would be a good thing.

I took another swig and a glint of metal swam in front of my vision. Grabbing my knife off the nightstand, I staggered to my feet and walked to the wall. Hundreds of little slashes marked the dingy grayed sheetrock. Vertical marks with a diagonal one across every four slashes. From as high as my arm could reach to my knees, there were hundreds of marks. Every seventy-three bundles I'd carved a crude box. Six boxes of seventy-three bundles and dozens of five stroke marks.

So many that I started counting.

Ten.

Twenty.

Fifty.

Seventy.

Oh God.

Seventy-one, seventy-two, seventy-three… Seventy-four, seventy-five…

It was no longer six years.

It was seven.

Seven years.

Seven years and two weeks.

"Tarquin," I cried on a sob, stabbing my knife into the wall and dragging it down, down, down, and over. "*Tarquin.*"

Seven fucking years.

No.

NO.

Not seven. Seven was the statute of limitation. This wasn't living. This wasn't jail. This wasn't a life.

This was hell.

HELL.

"No," I cried out, dragging the knife up and over. *"No!"* Driving the knife into the wall with one hand, I pounded on the sheetrock with my other. "NO," I screamed.

The door banged open.

"What the hell are you doing, girl?" Daddy snapped, coming at me.

Grabbing the hilt of the knife, I pulled it out of the wall. "Stay *the fuck* back!"

Two of Daddy's henchmen stepped in behind him.

Perfectly pressed jeans, no cut, reeking of aftershave and the devil, my disgusting excuse of a father crossed his arms. "You think you're going to what?" He laughed. "Stab me?"

"Fuck you!"

He tsked. *He fucking tsked.* Glancing over his shoulder, he nodded at one of the asshole bikers. "Get the pills."

My body shook, my guts turned, and I felt like I'd die if I didn't get more drugs. But for the first time in seven years, I didn't care. I wanted to be selfish. I *wanted* to die.

I couldn't do this.

No more.

"I ain't takin' more pills!" My arm shaking, I kept the knife between me and him.

Daddy smirked. "Right."

"You can't make me!"

"What are you gonna do, girl? Get sober?" Dripping sarcasm all over his last two words, he chuckled.

"Fuck you, I'm done."

His expression instantly morphed. Like I'd seen him do

a million times over, his face went blank, but I knew what I was looking at. I wasn't so far gone yet today that I didn't see the tightly controlled rage he managed to keep in check right before he killed somebody.

"And what exactly do you think you're done with, Shaila?"

"You can't keep me here anymore. I ain't doing this for him or you or nobody. I'm done, and I'm walkin' out that door."

Shocking the hell out of me, Daddy stepped aside. "Go ahead. Walk out," he taunted.

The two men behind him stepped aside too, but one of them smirked as he looked at the other.

I wasn't born yesterday. I didn't move.

"What's wrong, girl? Lost your bravery now?" He held his hand out toward the filthy, smoke-filled hallway of the clubhouse. "Walk."

Calling his bluff, I took a step.

"But know this," he clipped, dropping his voice to a deadly calm. "You step out that door, he dies." Leaning toward me, he delivered his final blow. "And so do his wife and children."

My stomach clenched, bile rose and my legs almost gave out.

Wife and children.

I stumbled back.

Wife and children.

My Tarquin.

Married.

Taking my own knife and stabbing myself would hurt a thousand times less than Daddy's ugly words.

"That's right," Daddy continued casually. "He's married, and he's happy. Want to know how many children he has? Children you couldn't give him."

I stumbled back another step, and my ass hit the wall.

The wall of years.

So many years.

He was happy.

Children.

I was a junkie whore.

He was a daddy.

"So what's it gonna be, girl?" The man who had fathered me sneered. "You walking out? You gonna decide his fate?"

Tarquin was a daddy.

Fisting my knife, I brought the blade to my left shoulder.

"Shaila," my father barked in warning.

Tarquin Scott was married.

I dragged the knife down diagonally across my body. Wet heat spread a second before searing pain stole my breath.

"*Jesus fucking Christ.*" Stone Hawkins lunged for me.

I stabbed the knife into my own stomach.

Chapter

ELEVEN

Candle

Rummaging through my supplies in the bathroom, I grabbed a couple quick clot bandages and pressed them to the wound on my shoulder. I'd had enough training in the Rangers and had been shot enough times to know I wasn't in danger of anything except infection and a painful recovery.

Pissed about my shoulder, pissed about the fucking mess in my living room, I gritted my teeth and pressed on the wound.

Her voice popped up in my head like it always did when I least expected it.

You don't go into the military without risk. That kinda life ain't no better than the club life.

My woman had been right. On both counts.

Feeling my cell vibrate in my pocket, I pulled it out and glanced at the display, but it was an unidentified number. I briefly considered ignoring it, but answered anyway. "What?"

"You haven't been out of jail an hour and you're already

neck-deep in trouble." Hawkins laughed. "Guess your little live-in girlfriend's secret is out of the bag. Who knew she was River Ranch?"

Wadding up my T-shirt, I pressed it over the quick clot bandage. "I hope you're hiding from me, motherfucker."

"Is that any way to talk to the one person who can destroy your life?"

My life was already destroyed, but I didn't give him the satisfaction of admitting to it. "Fair warning, I'm done. Call the Feds, call ATF, call whoever the fuck you want, I'm coming for you, Hawkins."

He made a tsking sound. "Just because everyone knows who your little brunette is now, doesn't mean you're off the hook with me. If you don't want the entire MC to be given orders by their president to bring her in, dead or alive, then you better listen—"

Rage hit, and I ate it up like a drug. "Give it your best shot, Hawkins. You're not getting at her or me. Your club imploded, you're in hiding, and the cartel wants you six feet under. You're already dead, motherfucker. DEAD."

He chuckled like he had the upper hand. "I just sent a text out. Better watch your back, Scott. And oh, your girlfriend's too."

"You know where you fucked up?" I didn't wait for him to answer. "Thinking you have loyalty." I hadn't been blindly doing his bidding for years while I worked on getting my shipment of Tavors stateside. I'd spent every fucking day I was under his thumb turning his members. I didn't get to them all, but I'd gotten to enough, and that was exactly why he had no fucking club left. "You better enjoy this moment, because it's one of the last ones you'll ever have." I hung up as someone pounded on the door to the garage.

Stepping around the fucking mess in my living room, I threw open the door.

Luna looked guilty, and Kendall was shaking.

"*Jesus fuck*," I muttered, glancing at Luna. "You fucking touched her back again." Would the prick ever learn?

"Oversight," he stated.

Tossing my bloody T-shirt down, I took her in my good arm. "Breathe it out, baby. Come on, you're stronger than this." I glanced at the clock on the wall in the garage.

"You're shot," she accused.

Fuck, I needed to get Link out of the front yard. "I'm okay."

She pulled away and looked at my shoulder. "You need to stop the bleeding."

"You need to get out of here," I countered.

She opened her mouth to give me shit, but I gripped her chin. Then I did what I hadn't done in fucking years. I reverted to compound speak. "*Decima*," I whispered so Luna didn't hear me. "Heed my warning. Take his shelter."

"Tarquin," she pleaded with fear in her eyes.

"He'll protect you better than I ever could." I dropped my hand and shut down my expression. "Leave. I'm dead to you." Without another word, I walked back into the house.

Pulling my phone out, I called Stripe.

He answered on the first ring, but his voice was low. "Need help cleaning up?"

"Can you get free without anyone noticing?" I glanced out the window as Luna pushed first Link's then Rip's bike into the garage.

"Yeah, but you gotta know something. Prez just sent a text. He wants Kendall, dead or alive. Fucker even said to kill you if we had to. Some of the guys are making plans now to come after you."

"Good. Let them." Then I wouldn't have to hunt them down to kill them. "She's gone now anyway." I watched Luna take one of my tarps, roll Link up and carry him to the garage before dumping him on the floor. Pulling gloves off, he got in the Jetta and drove away.

"They'll still find her," Stripe warned.

No, they wouldn't. Luna was good at what he did. And even if the few straggler bikers left over from our chapter caught up to them right now, they were no match for Luna and his men. Regardless, that didn't solve Kendall's problem or my promise to myself. I was done waiting for the perfect storm. I was going after River now.

"Alert the others who are on our side that we're going after River Stephens, but for fuck's sake, do it discreetly. If they balk at the two-million-dollar price tag they're giving up by leaving Kendall untouched, make sure they know River's full of shit. He won't pay up." I didn't know if he would or not. "Once we take River down, they can raid the compound for weapons."

"Copy that, I'll tell them."

Fucking dick, talking like he'd served. "Get over here once you handle that. I need cleanup help."

"Ten-four." Stripe hung up.

"Prick," I muttered.

Chapter TWELVE

Shaila

Sinking to the dirty floor, my body convulsed as unbearable pain robbed me of air.

"Pull the knife out," Daddy barked.

One of his henchmen dropped to his knee and hovered over me. "I can't do that. I think she hit something. She needs the hospital, Prez."

Shaking so bad I didn't know if I would lose my grip, I held the knife in my body as darkness crept at the edges of my vision. My hands wet, my body growing colder by the second, I silently begged for death.

"No one's going to the fucking hospital," Daddy snapped.

Our Father, who art in Heaven…

"She's losing a lot of blood."

Hallowed be Thy name…

"She's lost plenty of blood before and survived."

Thy Kingdom come…

"No disrespect, Prez, but if you want her to live, we

shouldn't pull that knife out. Not here. Not without something to stitch her up with, or at least stop the bleeding. And that's if she hasn't hit something major."

Thy will be done…

"I don't need a lecture. Do what I goddamn tell you to do."

On earth as it is in Heaven…

"Prez—"

"Pull the fucking knife out, or I'll stab you myself!"

A rough hand covered mine over the hilt and yanked.

A thousand points of blinding-hot pain hit my body all at once. My spine straightened, my mind snapped, my mouth opened and I convulsed. Then wet heat spread from my stomach, and my muscles curled.

"Deliver us from evil," I whisper-coughed.

"Fuck," the henchman cursed as metal clanked on the floor right before large hands pressed into my side. "*Fuck.*"

Blessed blackness took me.

Chapter
THIRTEEN

Candle

Stripe walked in the house over an hour later and glanced at my shoulder. "You okay?"

"Fine." This was nothing compared to getting shot on my first deployment. I was a fucking Ranger, for Christ's sake. *Sua Sponte*—of their own accord. Rangers lead the way. That's what I was taught, and that's what I was doing, wounded or not.

Not looking like he believed me, Stripe glanced at the tarp on the floor. "Smells like you had a party with bleach."

I kicked the tarp I'd rolled Rip up in. "Fucker bled all over the place. Help me carry him to the SUV."

"What are we doing with him?" Stripe picked one end up.

I grabbed the other end with my good arm. "We're taking him and Link to the Glades to Hawkins's property down there. We'll bury them, then burn the vehicle. How many LCs did you get to?" I should've called the fuckers myself, but I didn't want Stone getting word of this. I was hoping after we got River, I'd have a small army to go after Stone with, assuming one of those assholes knew where he was.

"Fifteen, maybe twenty, but I gotta tell you something, and you're not going to like it." He heaved his end of the tarp into the SUV that I'd back up into the garage, then he helped me grab my end.

"What?" My shoulder on fire despite the pain pills I'd taken, we shoved Rip in next to Link. Fuckers should've died seven years ago.

Stripe shut the lift gate and looked at me. "Prez didn't just put the call out locally to our chapter to bring Kendall in. He put it out to what's left of the entire club."

Mother. *Fucker.* "And you're just now telling me this?" I needed to up my timeline, immediately.

Stripe held his hands up. "You said no one would find her. I thought we had some time."

"Now we don't have time." Whipping my cell out, I dialed Kendall, but it went straight to voice mail. Fuck. I looked up the main number for Luna's office and called it.

"Luna and Associates," a brisk voice answered.

"This is Candle Scott. I need to speak with Luna immediately. Tell him I'm on the phone."

"Please hold."

A second later, that fuck Tyler picked up. "What's up, Scott?"

"Get Luna now is what's up."

"He's out of—"

"I didn't ask where the fuck he was. I told you to put me through to him. Tell him it's me and tell him it's urgent."

"Hang on." Tyler put me on hold.

Thirty seconds later, I heard the call go through. I didn't wait for Luna to speak. "I need to talk to Kendall, right fucking now."

"I'm here," Kendall answered.

"We're both here," Luna added.

"You didn't answer your phone, Kendall. Turn it the fuck on."

"Watch your tone, Ranger," Luna warned.

"Fuck you, Marine. Kendall, call me back, *privately*."

"I had the ringer turned off. What's going on?" Kendall asked, ignoring my order.

Jesus Christ. "Luna," I snapped. "Take me the fuck off speaker and give your phone to her."

"No can do," Luna clipped. "Tell us what's going on or I hang up."

Fuck, I didn't know what the hell she had or hadn't told him. But if he knew who Kendall was, he wouldn't be content with just getting her off the grid. He'd plan something, and I didn't want him in my way.

"Just say it," Kendall demanded.

"*Motherfucking shit.*" I knew Luna. He'd definitely go after River.

"Candle," Kendall snapped.

"Rip's a goddamn pussy, and I'm gonna bring him back to life so I can kill him all over again."

Neither of them said shit.

"Kendall." Fuck. She deserved better than this. My woman had deserved better too.

"It's okay, Candle," Kendall stated without an ounce of emotion.

No, it wasn't. I was pissed she'd been wearing that short-as-fuck nightgown, but the truth was, if I'd handled shit and shot Hawkins on sight that night in the Glades seven years ago, my woman might still be alive and Kendall wouldn't have an entire MC after her. "Goddamn it, baby, I'm fucking sorry." And I was. For everything.

"What did Rip do?" Luna asked.

"He talked," Kendall said, resigned.

"He didn't just talk," I corrected. "He sang like a fucking bird."

"To who?" Luna demanded, as if he knew what we were talking about.

"The whole goddamn club. I can't fucking contain this," I told Luna before addressing Kendall. "I can't kill everyone, Dee." Slipping, I used her real name, but she'd get the message that I was going after Stephens.

Luna cut in. "It's past time I know what the hell is going on, but I'm gonna let Kendall tell me that when we hang up. In the meantime, I'm assuming her safety is compromised."

"Good fucking assumption." Prick.

"Drop the fucking attitude, Scott, and tell me how much time I have."

He hadn't seen my attitude yet. "As long as it takes for an entire MC chapter to track her car to the airport, asshole. Then they'll hold a gun to the head of some minimum-wage desk fuck until he tells them your flight plan. After that, they'll tear up the road getting to you. You do the math. Three, four hours if you're lucky."

Luna swore in Spanish. "Then what?"

"Then they kill her for the bounty on her head."

"How much?" Luna demanded.

"Dead or alive?"

"There's a difference?" he asked.

A big fucking difference. "One million alive. Two if it's just her head." And Luna better fucking protect her head and everything else about her like he'd said he would until I got to Stephens, because I wasn't having another woman's death on my hands. "If a single fucking hair on her head is harmed, I am holding you responsible. I will hunt you down, Luna, and I will fucking cut you. Do you understand me?"

"Calm the fuck down. Did Rip know who I was?"

This was my calm. "I don't know what the fuck he knew, but her car is known, and it won't take long to figure out who flew you two out of here."

"How many members are still left in your chapter?" he asked.

"It's not my chapter you have to worry about. The Lone Coasters have chapters up and down the East Coast, and everyone's poor as fuck right now. They'll jump on that two million."

"What are you doing at your end?"

I had to give Luna credit, he didn't ask the question as an accusation. He asked like he was merely asking for a sitrep. But I still wasn't going to tell him my plan. Instead I gave him the simple facts. "I've been locked up six months. What's left of my chapter has fucking imploded or gone rogue." And I was going to use that to my advantage.

"Fine. I'll handle it. Where can I reach you?"

Handle my ass. "She has my number."

"Copy that." His tone went all business. "I'll be in touch."

I didn't like the sound of that. "Luna."

"What?"

"Just get her out of town. Give me a week or two. I'll discredit Rip." No way in hell was I waiting two days, let alone two weeks, but I needed to throw Luna off. When Stephens was dead, it wouldn't matter who knew Kendall's real identity.

"I'll handle it," Luna repeated.

"You don't have enough manpower to go up against the LCs," I warned.

"What I lack in head count, I make up for in training. Make some calls on your end. Find out how far this has spread. Get back to me in an hour." Luna hung up.

I shoved my cell back in my pocket.

Stripe raised an eyebrow. "Problems with Luna?"

"No." Maybe.

Stripe frowned. "What's our plan?"

"Kill River Stephens, then Hawkins." Heading back into the house, I went to my gun safe in the master bedroom closet. Grabbing my rifle, a shotgun, a 9mm, and a shit ton of ammo, I placed it on a shelf before locking the safe again.

Stripe glanced at my firepower. "How are we gonna get to Stephens?"

I shoved my 9mm in my back waistband and hefted the two other guns. "Ride to the compound gates and start shooting. Grab the ammo."

Stripe was a lot of things, but self-thinking wasn't one of them. "That'll work?"

"Yeah." It had to. I grabbed more bandages and the painkillers before walking to the garage and tipping my chin at the saddlebag on my Road King. "Put the ammo in there."

"What about Stone?" Stripe asked as he stowed the ammo. "He's not telling anyone where he is, and the only people who might've known for sure where he's hiding are in there." Stripe nodded toward the SUV.

"I'll find Stone." If it was the last thing I did. "River first." I secured the rifle and the shotgun to mounts I had installed on my bike. Then I grabbed a spare gas can from the garage and headed toward the SUV.

Stripe took the can from me and put it in the SUV. "Okay, River first," he agreed, nodding like none of this was a suicide mission. "Then are you going to regroup the club?"

"No." *Hell fucking no.* "But when the dust settles, have at it." My shoulder killing me, I handed the SUV's keys to him, then straddled my hog. "Keep up."

Chapter Fourteen

Candle

Driving down a road I never wanted to be on, I averted my eyes from a house I didn't want to see as I pulled behind the garage on Hawkins's property where my woman had hiddn me a lifetime ago.

Stripe stopped the SUV next to my Road King and hopped out. "I made calls on the drive down to confirm we had head count. We've got twenty-three, including you and me. I told everyone to meet us here before first light tomorrow and we'd hit the compound then. Good?"

Trying not to look at the fucking house where my woman died, I nodded as I walked toward the back of the SUV.

Following me, Stripe frowned. "I can make a few more calls, maybe get a couple more guys?"

"We're good." We weren't good. There were hundreds of armed fucks at River Ranch. "Let's get the bodies out of the SUV. Then we'll dump the vehicle and come back to bury these assholes."

"Ten-four." Stripe pulled the tarp-wrapped bodies out.

My shoulder killing me, I headed back to my bike. "Follow me."

With Stripe on my six, I drove to a shit industrial part of Miami where we wiped down the SUV and set it on fire. Then I took us back to the Glades and was on my fourth pain pill and second set of bandages when Stripe finally had enough sense to get concerned.

"Think they'll find evidence in that SUV? I mean, like my DNA or something?"

The shallow grave dug, the bodies in it, we were already piling the dirt back on.

"No." I held my shovel one handed as Stripe worked twice as fast as me. "That's why we torched it." I threw another shovelful of dirt, and my cell pinged with a text.

I glanced at the screen.

Kendall: *Answer your phone.*

A second later, my cell rang with a call from an unidentified number.

I swiped my thumb across the screen. "What's up?"

"There're LCs as far south as Homestead," Luna accused. "You're not containing this."

"I'm working on it," I lied.

"Work harder."

About to pass the fuck out, I gave up lifting the shovel and started pushing it like a goddamn snowplow. "Get off the fucking road."

"I'm not on the road."

"Jesus fuck." I could hear traffic in the background. "Just get her somewhere safe until I handle this."

"You're in over your head," he uselessly warned.

I pushed more dirt toward the grave. "What the fuck do you know about it?"

Luna paused a fraction of a second. "Everything."

"*Christ.* She fucking told you?"

"Handle your end." Luna ignored my question. "I'm working on a plan."

"No, you're fucking not. Don't do a goddamn—"

Luna hung up.

Jamming my cell back in my pocket, I swatted a fucking mosquito. "When's everyone getting here again?"

Stripe patted the dirt with the back of his shovel. "I told them before dawn."

Shit. That may not be soon enough to get a jump on whatever the hell Luna was planning, which was probably a version of what I was doing, except he'd have trained men and more ammo. For a second, I thought about combining forces but quickly dismissed it. I wanted River dead, not in jail, and from everything I'd heard about Luna, he was by the book. "Any way to up the timeline?"

Stripe shrugged. "Yeah, I guess, but it'd mean fewer numbers. I got some guys coming from the Jacksonville chapter. They won't get here till go time."

Maybe I'd underestimated Stripe. "How the fuck did you manage that?"

He smirked. "You weren't the only one all these years going around Hawkins's back. While you were busy working the shop, ignoring every brother who wasn't two inches in front of you, I was scouting."

Christ. "They loyal? More importantly, can they shoot?"

"Yep and yep." He smiled. "So we should wait for them."

Not bothering to argue because he was right, I started back toward the garage.

Stripe fell in step beside me and nodded at the house. "We should wait in there and get out of this heat. Looks like it has AC."

I stopped dead in my tracks. "No," I bit out. "No one goes in that house, you hear me? Any asshole who steps foot in there, I will *fucking* shoot."

Eyebrows raised, Stripe held his hands up. "Okay, okay. But it's a waste of good AC, if you ask me."

"I mean it," I warned.

"I hear you." Stripe held his hands up a moment longer, then slowly lowered them. "Garage it is."

Fuming, I walked into the garage, and memories hit me like a fucking fifty-caliber bullet. Everywhere I looked, I saw her. But gone was the neatly swept floor and organized piles of shit people collected in a garage. There was no air mattress, or Spam sandwiches or bottle of liquid soap with a hose dragged into the middle of the space. A layer of dust now coated everything, mingling with the overpowering scent of rotten wood.

I barely spared Stripe a glance. "I'm getting some rest."

"Copy that." Pulling his cell out, he sat on the floor against the wall. "I'm gonna have my woman pick me up and take me back to get my ride. But don't worry, I'll be back before everyone else gets here."

Fuck. "You have an old lady?" Now I'd think twice if I had to kill him.

He smiled wide. "Yep. Dannie. We been together since before I prospected."

"She know about club life?" I fished.

His smile dropped, and for once he looked threatening. "Don't even think it. She's not going to tell anyone about anything. She's not a snitch."

Nodding, I walked over to the bench I'd taken my woman on.

Taken.

Not fucked.

Because that's what I'd done. I'd taken her virginity, then I took her life as sure as I'd pushed her off that porch myself, because her death was my fault. I didn't protect her. And in a few hours, I was going to kill the man who'd inadvertently brought her into my life.

Life wasn't short. It was bullshit and irony.

I sat down, leaned against the bench and closed my eyes.

Chapter FIFTEEN

Shaila

One second I was floating, the next I was drowning in hurt.

My side, my chest, my arms, my legs. Shallow breaths not filling my lungs, I tried to inhale deep, and excruciating pain lanced up my side. Crying out, I blindly reached for pills that should've been on the nightstand.

"Fuck, she's coming to. Hold her down," a deep voice barked.

Pressure hit my upper arms, and my hand grasped at air. "Pills," I groaned.

"Hurry up," another voice ordered. "Get those stitches in."

The second I heard the word stitches, it all came rushing back.

Seven years.

Daddy.

The knife.

Seven fucking years.

"No," I cried out. I didn't want stitches. I didn't want to be fixed up. I didn't want to live.

But big hands held my arms down as someone tugged by my stab wound.

"No." I kicked out, and pain worse than when I'd driven the knife into my own flesh ripped through my side and radiated. "Stop! Let me die!"

The slap was so unexpected, my head whipped to the side. Then a rough hand gripped my chin with enough force to break bones.

My eyes popped open.

Seething mad, Daddy glared at me. "I'm only going to say this once, so listen up, girl. You will lie there and you will get your stitches. Then I'm giving you a week. One goddamn week, and you will go back to working this club and doing whatever you're told. You hear me?"

"Fuck you," I spat.

Daddy slapped me again, but a hundred times harder.

Blood pooled in my mouth, my teeth rattled, and I momentarily saw stars.

Then something happened.

The stars cleared, the hurt receded, and a fog lifted.

I wasn't angry.

I wasn't in pain.

I didn't care about the man stitching me or the seven lost years… or even him.

I didn't care.

Daddy grabbed my chin again in a punishing grip. "You will do what I say, when I say it. You will always do what I say." Barely contained fury in his voice and in his eyes, he paused for effect. *"I own you."*

I. Did. Not. *Care.*

"No. You don't. Not anymore." Then I said something I should've said seven years ago. "Kill me." Despite his hold on me, I raised my head. "Because if you don't, I'll do it myself."

With sickening force, his palm connected with my cheek again.

A smile spread across my face.

His nostrils flared, and the man I used to call Daddy grabbed my hand and slapped a handcuff over my wrist before closing the other cuff around the metal bar of the headboard.

Straightening to his full height, his expression did a one-eighty. His features smoothed out, and he smiled down at me.

I own you, he mouthed.

"Liar," I whispered.

Stone Nathanial Hawkins winked at me. "We'll see." Then he dropped the charade and glanced at the asshole still holding my arms down. "Keep her chained up. One week. I don't give a fuck if she pisses in the bed. Then uncuff her and put her back to work."

The asshole whose name I had never bothered to learn, but who had used me just the same as all the other biker assholes in this place, gave Stone a look of concern.

Stone's hands went to his hips as his voice dropped to a deadly polite tone. "Do you have something to say?"

The asshole sealed his fate. "One week isn't enough time to heal from a stab wound like that."

Stone Hawkins raised an eyebrow. "Is her cunt broken? Is she incapable of spreading her legs?"

The tugging on my side stopped. "Stitches all in," the

other asshole announced. "If she doesn't kick around, they'll hold."

Stone ignored the second asshole and spoke to the first. "What's your name, son?"

"Burner, sir. I'm a welder. I know I'm no doctor, but she doesn't look—"

"I believe I asked you a question, Burner," Stone interrupted. "Two actually. Are you going to answer them?"

"Look, I understand what you're getting at. All I'm saying is—"

Stone Hawkins pulled his gun out and shot him dead.

With a hole in the middle of his forehead, Burner hit the floor with a thud, and the scent of gunpowder filled the small room.

Stone glanced at the asshole who'd stitched me up. "Take out the trash. Leave her cuffed, and make sure she doesn't cut herself again."

The asshole didn't even blink. "Sure thing, boss."

Stone Hawkins walked out of the room.

Chapter SIXTEEN

Candle

With the roar of twenty-two bikes idling behind me, and the sun coming up, I glanced over my shoulder. The men behind me weren't Rangers. They weren't even military worthy.

But they were the army I had.

"No shooting women or children," I shouted over the noise of the pipes. "Got it?"

Head nods, chin tips, and revved engines were my affirmations, and I took it, but it was bullshit. I knew this was going to be a bloodbath. For that reason, I didn't give the warning that River was mine or bother saying I wanted him taken alive so I could kill him myself.

I no longer gave a fuck who pulled the trigger.

This wasn't a seven-year-old vendetta for revenge anymore. This was taking the fucking trash out. This was eliminating Kendall's bounty. This was delivering every damn River Ranch member from evil. River Stephens needed to be dead.

Kicking my bike into gear, I nodded once at the men behind me, then I revved the engine and released the clutch.

My Harley chewing up the miles, I led us to River Ranch. Twenty minutes later, we were turning down the road to the compound. Grabbing my shotgun from its mount, I drove around the final bend leading to the front gates.

I was expecting to feel adrenaline. I was expecting to see an armed guard on gate duty. I was expecting to feel rage...

I wasn't expecting was open compound gates, a half-empty panel truck with crates of guns and two black Luna and Associates SUVs.

Motherfucker.

Giving my bike gas, I sped through the open chain-link gate, slammed on the brakes and aimed my shotgun single-handed at the main building of River Ranch as Luna and a few of his men scrambled.

"River," I yelled. "Get the fuck out here!"

Ignoring Luna's deadly glare, I scanned the compound at warp speed. No River and no compound fucks in sight, but I knew they were there just past the tree line, aiming their shit weapons at us.

Before I could yell again for River to show his fucking face, a shot came from the woods and plunked off the panel truck.

For a blink, no one fired back.

Then all hell broke loose.

Luna hit the ground. He and his men started firing, I dropped behind my bike, and the LCs all started unloading. One of Luna's black SUVs reversed, then lurched forward, and angled between the panel truck and me and the rest of the bikers.

Heavy gunfire raining down from every goddamn direction, I kept my eye on the front building where River's office was.

I needed inside.

But I needed cover fire to get there, and every goddamn biker was blindly firing like this was the fucking Alamo. Just as I glanced behind me for Stripe, the same SUV that'd moved before suddenly floored it.

The Escalade slammed into River Ranch's main building.

And kept going.

Chapter
SEVENTEEN

Shaila

The asshole still living walked into the bathroom and came back out with a wet towel.

Eyeing his movements, my body started to tremble from cold or shock, I didn't know which. "That's not gonna be big enough to clean up a dead body."

"Not using it for that." No emotion in his tone, he leaned over me and wiped my side.

At first the warm, wet towel felt like a godsend, but then the pressure of his touch stabbed at my wound. Gritting my teeth, I didn't give him the satisfaction of crying out in pain. Instead, I aimed for dissension amongst Stone's ranks.

"You know he'll shoot you one day. Just like he shot Mr. Disagreement."

The asshole made a sound low in his throat that could've been him agreeing or disagreeing.

"Is that how you wanna die? A bullet between the eyes?"

"We all gotta go sometime." He wiped harder.

I couldn't help it. I grunted.

He smiled as he stood upright, but he didn't make eye contact. Then he whipped the sheet out from under me in one fast, hard yank.

My body rolled toward my wound, the handcuff cut into my flesh, and pain ripped through my side.

"You motherfucker!" I cried out.

The asshole started whistling and rolling the dead biker up in my sheet.

Panting through the pain, wishing I'd done more than just drag the knife across my torso when I'd had the chance, I gingerly rolled to my back. Nothing to be done about my wrist, my arm hung there as it started to go pins and needles.

The psycho whistling biker finished rolling up the dead biker. Hefting the body over his shoulder, he headed for the door.

"Hey, you can't leave me like this." Naked, shaking, and in pain, I couldn't lay here all night like this.

"Can and will." The asshole didn't even glance at me.

"Wait." *Damn it.* "I can't just lie here naked. I need to treat the wound across my chest. I need to use the bathroom and wash it." And drink a bottle of tequila. And find some pills.

"You should've thought about that before you took a knife to yourself." He walked out the door, kicking it shut behind him.

Shit.

My left arm handcuffed above my head, my sheet gone, my body shaking, I dared to look down at myself.

Shit.

The bright red welt ran from the top of my left breast

and crossed down to my right hip. Not deep enough to need stitches, blood crusted in places and oozed in others. But the stab wound on my right side, above my hip and in an inch, was an angry red and inflamed, and three black Xs of crude stitches were holding the cut closed.

Reaching out with a trembling hand, I touched the top stitch.

Flinching, I sucked in a sharp breath as pain ate up my side like a rabid animal. "Sweet Jesus," I muttered, but then I laughed at my own stupidity. Stomach muscles I never knew I used recoiled at the sudden movement of my wounded body, and my laugh turned into a cry of pain.

"Shit," I panted as a hot flash heated my face.

There wasn't no such thing as Jesus and nothing about him would be sweet if there were. God didn't live in this hell, and I was stupid for ever believing in him. Life ain't got no mercy for the whore daughter of a murderer.

A whore daughter too stupid to kill herself when she had the chance.

Now I was chained up like a dog.

A pathetic, drug-addicted, alcoholic, whoring dog.

Yanking on my handcuffed arm, I cussed as the metal clanked against the headboard.

But then I saw it.

My knife.

Bloodied and lying on the floor not two feet from the bed.

"Come on, girl," I whispered. "You can do this."

Panting short and shallow, hoping it would quell the pain, I used my unchained arm to push myself into a sitting position. My body screamed, my limbs shook harder, and sweat broke out across my brow.

I didn't care.

I scooted my ass to the very edge of the bed as far as my handcuffed arm would let me. Then I took as deep a breath as I could and held it.

Extending my left leg, I reached out with my foot.

My toe touched cold metal.

Chapter EIGHTEEN

Candle

The SUV ripped through the wood building like an IED. Then a second later, the other black SUV gunned it and followed suit.

Wood cracked, glass shattered, and the roof fell in. Men started yelling as gunfire rang out from inside the fucking destruction of what was left of the main building.

But outside the firing stopped.

Completely.

Then one by one, River Ranch men started spilling out of the bushes like ants. Eyes wide, faces drawn, their weapons were down. Staring at the ruins that used to be their leader's headquarters, they looked like the fucking apocalypse of lost souls.

The gunfire stopped from inside the wreckage, a cloud of dust rose from the gaping hole that used to be the front of the building, and lights flickered.

Then I heard Luna yell. "Chica, no!"

A single gunshot echoed from inside, and I was moving.

Before I crossed the distance to the building, Kendall was rushing out. Debris in her hair, tears streaming down her face, she ran right past me.

A second later, that Tyler fuck came out after her. "Which way did she go?"

"To your left," a deep, accented voice said from my six.

I looked over my shoulder.

Fucking Neil Christensen. Former Danish Special Forces, friend of Luna's and all-around asshole.

"Copy that." Tyler ran off.

Christensen and another guy who looked like he killed for sport stepped past me.

Christensen spared me a glance. "Your approach was sloppy, and your timing was off." His eyes darted to my shoulder then back to me. "That would not have happened if you had used your training." He and the other asshole walked into the wreckage.

Fucking dick.

"Candle," Stripe called, running up to me then lowering his voice. "Jesus, these guys are like fucking zombies. They're freaking me out. What the hell are they doing?"

"Not now." Brushing him off, I followed Christensen.

Holding my shoulder as blood seeped through my shirt, I stepped over the rubble and into the pile of debris that used to be River's office. Dead compound men lay scattered in the wreckage as Luna, Talon Talerco, Christensen, the guy with him, another guy I'd never seen and Hero, one of the compound's hunters, all stood in a half circle around a desk.

Behind the desk, lying on the floor with his face practically blown off, was River Stephens.

For two whole seconds, I stared at the piece of shit who'd had me beaten and stabbed and thrown out of the only home I'd ever known.

I'd thought I would feel satisfaction.

I didn't feel a goddamn thing.

"Good," I clipped. "He's fucking dead."

Faster than I could blink, Luna surged.

His fist made solid contact with my face before I could turn my head, and the asshole broke my fucking nose. My shoulder already shot, taken off guard, I hit the ground. The fucker got three more punches in before Talerco pulled him off.

"Patrol," Talerco barked at Luna. "Go take care of your woman."

Spitting fucking mad, Luna kicked me.

"All right." I threw a hand up. "I fucking get it, asshole." He was pissed I'd rained on his parade. The feeling was mutual. "But he's dead, which is more than you were fucking doing." So he needed to get the fuck over it.

Holding Luna by the arms, Talon yanked him back a foot. "You fuckin' taunt him again, and I'm gonna let go of him just so I can kick you myself."

"ATF is on their way," Neil interrupted.

"Come on, Patrol." Talon dragged Luna toward the passenger door of one of the trashed SUVs. "Let's roll."

The guy I'd never seen before silently got behind the wheel of the second SUV and started backing out.

"I need to contain this," Luna clipped.

"I will handle it. Leave," Neil ordered.

"My prints, my guns, my vehicles, I'm all over this fucking thing," Luna bitched.

Christensen ignored Luna, and Talon shoved him into the first SUV's front passenger seat. "Let Vikin' do his thing." Talon rounded the vehicle, got behind the wheel and reversed out.

My shoulder on fire, my nose bleeding, I got up as the guy who'd walked in with Christensen checked for a pulse on one of the bodies lying in the rubble, then moved on to the next body.

Christensen glanced at his phone, then sent a text.

A foot taller than I remembered and a hell of a lot more ripped, Hero looked at me. "I thought you were dead."

I wasn't that fucking lucky. "Not yet." I glanced at the rifle in his hand, then Stephens's corpse. No handgun had done that to his face. "You kill him?"

Hero didn't hesitate. "I did what needed to be done."

Respecting his answer, I nodded. Then I gave him the only thing I had to give. "Thanks for taking care of Decima after I was gone."

His expression already reticent, he gave nothing away. "I thought she was deceased as well."

"Yeah, well, she wasn't."

The guy with Christensen suddenly turned back to the first body he'd checked and fired a single shot.

A gun fell out of the River Ranch brother's hand.

Christensen put his phone away and looked at me. "You and your men leave. You have seven minutes."

"They're not going to want to leave empty-handed." I saw the crates in the panel truck as I'd driven in. I could tell by the size and shape of them that they weren't Tavors, but they were some kind of firepower.

Neil eyed me a moment. "Three crates."

"Six," I countered.

"Five. And you now have six minutes."

"Done." Nodding at Hero, I walked out.

His 9mm in his hand, Stripe stood outside the wrecked building. "We good? He dead?"

"Yeah." I glanced at all the compound brothers standing silent, waiting for orders that would never come from a leader they would never see again. I looked back at Stripe. "You and the guys can take five crates of the weapons on the panel truck, but hurry the fuck up. ATF will be here in six minutes."

"Copy that, on it, Sarge."

I leveled Stripe with a look. "I'm not your Sarge. I'm no one to you now."

He blinked.

"Go. You're out of time." I turned toward where I'd left my bike.

"Wait. What about Hawkins?" Stripe asked.

"I'm going after him alone." I didn't wait for a protest or argument from him. I walked to my Road King and prayed like fuck it wasn't too shot up to start.

It wasn't.

Throwing a leg over, I hit the kickstand and shifted into gear.

Without looking back, I drove away from my past.

Chapter Nineteen

Shaila

Sweating, shaking, all at once hot and cold, my toes curled around the hilt of my knife.

Come on, come on, come on, I silently chanted.

Don't screw up. Don't let go. Don't rush.

Don't drop the knife.

Slow, I dragged my foot with the knife underneath toward the bed.

"Yes," I whispered. "Almost… *almost.*"

My muscles nonexistent, my toes slipped.

Shit.

Straining against the handcuff, my stab wound screaming, my leg extended beyond comfort, I toed the knife again and slowly pulled it all the way to the edge of the bed.

Panting as if I'd run a mile, I carefully took my foot off the hilt and sat a moment.

Chained to the headboard, I couldn't just lean down and pick up the knife, and the handle was too wide to grasp between the toes of one foot. Scooting back, I tested to see if

I lay on my stomach, if my free arm could reach the floor. My wound throbbing, I gave it shot, but I couldn't stretch far enough.

Fuck.

My only other option was to use both my feet to pick it up. The last thing I wanted to do was use my stomach muscles to lift my legs, but I didn't have a choice. I didn't know when the asshole who'd stitched me would come back, and I sure as hell wasn't going to wait here and see what the next week brought.

Knowing I couldn't stall any longer, I psyched myself up. "Just fuckin' do it, Shaila. Ain't nobody gonna save you." I sat up again and ignored the wave of nausea from the pain. "Just…" I put both feet on the floor. "Fuckin'…" I pinched the knife between my toes. "Do it!" I lifted my legs.

Motherfucking shit goddamn it.

"Gaaaahhhhh."

My whole body shaking like I was convulsing, my legs swung up and the knife dropped on the mattress a split second before my legs fell on top of it.

"Fuckin' *shit*, that hurts." Curling onto my good side, I used my left leg to shove the knife up toward me. My fingers touched the hilt and the door to my room banged open.

Blood on his shoulder and his cheek, the asshole who'd stitched me up walked in.

I panicked.

No sheet, no clothes, I had nowhere to hide the knife. If he saw it was gone from the floor, I was completely screwed.

Think, Shaila, *think.*

Grasping at distraction, I nodded toward the broken

dresser that had pitifully few clothes. "I'm cold and cut. You can't leave me naked and my wounds uncovered. I'll die from infection before the week's out. See what your precious Prez thinks of you then if you let his daughter die."

Exactly how I prayed he would, he glanced over his shoulder at the dresser.

I quickly slid the knife under my pillow.

When the asshole looked back at me, he smirked. "Club whores don't need clothes."

I hated him and I wanted him dead. "Unwounded club whores not in shock don't need clothes."

He smirked. "You're not in shock. You're shaking because you got the DTs."

Asshole. "Get me a shirt."

"How about I do you one better." He kicked the door shut, then he walked over to the edge of the bed. His crazy eyes on me, he pulled a bottle of pills out of his jeans pocket and set it on the far side of the nightstand. Just out of reach.

I knew I was jonesing.

I was in horrible, mind-bending pain, and shit was radiating from my stab wound, and I was probably already sporting an infection from his dirty stitches, but the second I saw that bottle, I was a whole lot worse off.

I wanted those pain killers.

And not just two fucking pills.

I wanted *all* the pills. Because I had no self-control. Which was why I was in here now, stabbed and looking at a little orange bottle with a blue lid and praying to that bottle's contents like it was salvation itself.

Which they were.

Those pills were the only way I'd survived seven years of hell.

But then it hit me.

A thought so obvious and so profound that I couldn't believe I was so, *so* stupid for not seeing it before. And once I saw it, I couldn't unsee it.

Those pills were *why* I'd been here seven years.

I wasn't a prisoner of Stone fucking Hawkins.

I wasn't locked up in this dirty MC clubhouse.

I wasn't forced to stay in this room day in and day out.

No one had chained me up before tonight.

I was here because I chose to be here.

I chose those pills.

I'd fucking reached for them each and every time they'd been offered to me, and I'd eaten them up like candy. I may not have willingly taken them the first few times Stone had fed them to me, but I'd sure as hell taken 'em after that.

I'd even chased them with tequila. And vodka, and beer, and whiskey and anything else I could get my hands on.

But I could've not taken them.

I could've pretended to take them, then spit them out.

I could've saved them up and when I had a whole bottle's worth, I could've taken them all at once and ended this farce of a life.

But I hadn't, and now here I was, staring at that bottle, literally shaking with want.

I'd turned into my mother.

My teeth chattered, my hands trembled and nausea twisted my stomach.

I knew what I had to do.

"Get me a shirt," I demanded.

The asshole snorted. "How you gonna put it on?"

I fought not to cuss at him. "You're gonna uncuff me long enough so I can pull it over my head and arm."

Evil and disturbing, he smiled. "Am I now?"

In that moment, I was thankful he'd never been one of the regulars who'd come up to my room. Although, I'd passed out so many times, who the hell could be sure. He looked like the kind of sick fuck that'd do exactly that, take a woman who was unconscious. The thought making me shake harder, I shoved it down and focused on what I needed to do.

Changing my tactic, I put a heaping dose of pathetic into my tone. "It's just a shirt," I pleaded. "Please?"

Not taking his creepy eyes off me, he reached behind him, yanked a drawer open and grabbed the first thing his hand landed on.

He tossed me a tank top.

My left hand on my knife under the pillow, I had no choice. I reached for the shirt with my right hand. My stab wound exploded with a fresh wave of pain and I sucked in a sharp before quickly dropping my arm.

My whole body trembling, my voice shook. "P-p-please help me." I held the tank up a couple inches.

The asshole unbuckled his jeans. "Yeah, I'm gonna help you, bitch." He stepped toward the bed as he fisted his dick. "Right after you help me." Grabbing a handful of my hair, he yanked my head to the side. "Open your mouth and make this good. If you swallow every fucking drop, I'll give you a pill."

"W-w-wait." *Not yet, girl, not yet.* "I need to tell you something first."

He brought his nasty dick to my face. "Then say it."

Steady girl, steady. "Come closer," I whispered, forcing my jaw not to chatter. "Bring your face to mine."

He snorted in disgust. "Your mouth's not touching mine."

"No kissin', I promise." I didn't kiss any of them. Not in seven years. "I just wanna look in your eyes and say somethin'." My expression perfect, I played my part. "Please," I whispered.

Gripping my hair tighter, he leaned down and got in my face. "What could a club whore possibly say to me that I would want to hear?"

Whipping my hand out, blade first, I drove my knife into his neck. "Die, motherfucker."

His eyes popped wide with shock, blood spurted, his mouth opened, and he made a half gurgling, half choking sound. Releasing his hold on my hair, he reached for the knife.

I twisted the handle.

Blood coming out of his mouth, his knees gave out.

I yanked the knife out, and he hit the floor.

My heart slamming against my chest, my hand covered in hot, sticky blood, I brought the knife to my handcuffed wrist. Shoving the tip of the blade between the paw and the swing arm like the man who'd fathered me taught me, I held the knife just so. The paw released the swing, and I pulled my wrist free.

Scrambling to get up, my feet hit the floor and I stepped in blood.

I didn't care.

I was already reaching for the pills.

Dropping the knife, grabbing the bottle, I stepped over the asshole and aimed for the bathroom. My hands shaking, the pills rattled. Leaving a bloody handprint on the faucet, I turned the water on. Opening the bottle and bringing it to my lips, I didn't even count.

I tipped the bottle back.

My mouth filled with pills, and I held my face under the faucet.

Then I swallowed every single painkiller.

Chapter
TWENTY

Candle
Four weeks later.
Ormond Beach, Florida.

Tossing the drink back, I slammed the shot glass on the bar and reached in my back pocket for my wallet. The fucking gunshot wound in my shoulder still healing, I felt every goddamn inch of the stretch.

The brunette bartender leaned on the bar, giving me an eyeful of her tits. "That's all you're gonna have, soldier?"

"Who says I'm a soldier?" I wasn't a Ranger anymore.

"Sailor?" she asked flirtatiously.

"Fuck, no." I tossed a twenty on the bar. "Keep the change."

"I'd like to keep you." She winked.

Only because her tits were fucking huge, I didn't bite her head off. "I'm not for keeps, sweetheart."

"So I was right." She swiped the money.

Jesus. "About?"

She grinned. "Army."

Fucking uniform junkie. I hated them. "Tell you what." I leaned forward and waited.

She pressed her rack against the bar to get closer to me. Dropping her voice, she licked her lips. "Yes?"

Using my good arm, I fisted a handful of her long hair. "You tell me exactly what I did in the Army, and I'll let you suck my dick."

She grinned like she had me. "Green Beret."

I immediately released her. "Fuck no."

"*Shit.*" She shook her head. "I knew I should've said Ranger."

"You should've said biker," a voice interrupted.

I looked up. Fucking André Luna. "You lost? Miami's four hours south."

"Don't I know it." Prick sat down next to me and nodded at the bartender. "I'll have whatever he's having."

"Water," I clipped at the bartender. I wasn't drinking with this asshole.

Luna chuckled. "Water it is."

The bartender filled two glasses and set them in front of us. "Another hot military soldier. I like it."

"Marine, chica," Luna corrected. "But thanks for the compliment."

"Plenty more where that came from, *Marine.*" She winked at him.

"I'm sure, chica, but save it for a man who's worthy. And single," he added.

The bartender laughed. "Smooth, Marine. And point taken. Come find me if your woman ever gets tired of you."

"Not gonna happen, but thanks anyway." Luna smiled.

"Can't blame a girl for trying." Shrugging, the bartender moved on to the next customer.

I drank the water. "What are you doing here?"

Scanning the bar, Luna glanced at the exit twice. "My woman says I need to forgive you for almost getting her killed."

I snorted. I knew he had it bad for her. "You taking orders from Kendall now?"

"No, I just thought I'd come up here and beat the shit out of you again, then tell her we made up."

"First of all, you didn't beat the shit out of me. You hit like a fucking pussy. Second of all, I wasn't the asshole who delivered Kendall to fucking River Ranch when Stephens had a goddamn bounty on her head. You going after Stephens with a handful of Marines was fucking amateur. At least I brought a couple dozen trigger-happy bikers." Numbers were numbers.

Luna lifted a shoulder as he drank his water. "You have your ways. I have mine."

"And neither of us got to Stephens. It was his own damn hunter who pulled the trigger."

"No skin off my back. The pendejo is dead."

Seven years in the making to get at Stephens, and I didn't get to pull the trigger. Worse, I no longer cared. My sole focus was Stone Hawkins, but I couldn't find him anywhere.

Turning on his stool to face me, Luna frowned. "You know what I can't figure out?"

"How you allowed yourself to get pussy whipped?" He didn't stand a chance against Kendall. She'd called me a dozen times since the compound raid, but I'd ignored all her calls.

Since she hadn't shown back up at my house, I figured all was good.

Luna kept talking like I gave a fuck. "I can't figure out how you hooked up with Stone Hawkins in the first place."

Every muscle tensed, and I locked my expression down. "I'm just a lucky guy."

"Here's the thing." He eyed me for a moment. "I don't think it was. I think it was something more." He set his water down. "I think you crawled out of that swamp in the Glades and stumbled onto his property. I think you found the house he used to keep his old lady at."

I drank another sip of water. "What do you want, Luna? I got shit to do."

"The Israeli guns you bought downrange and brought back to fence were confiscated. The auto shop you ran for Hawkins was shut down seven months ago when you went to jail for assault. The Lone Coasters MC has disintegrated. Stone Hawkins is in the wind, and River Stephens is dead." He rattled off the events of my life like he was reading a goddamn résumé. "What the fuck do you have left to do?"

Anger surged, and I glared at Luna. "Kill Hawkins."

Luna raised an eyebrow. "And you're waiting for what exactly?"

Pissed off, tired, and frustrated, I slipped and showed my hand. "I'm waiting till I fucking find him."

Turning to face forward again, Luna casually picked up his water. "Good luck doing that on your own."

"Fuck off."

"Tell me why you want him dead."

"No."

"Tell me and I'll help you find him," he offered.

"Still no." Trying to shove every shit thing in my life down deep, I stared out at the ocean across the street.

Slow and practiced, Luna nodded. "All right. I get it."

He didn't get shit. Not even I knew why I was turning down his help at this point, other than he could implicate me if it ever came down to that. But no Feds had come after me for the shit at the compound, so that should've been a good enough sign I could trust him, but I didn't. Not entirely. So I sat there and said nothing, and neither did he.

For a full three minutes.

Then Luna glanced at me and took a wild stab. "Was it Hawkins's old lady?"

"What the fuck are you talking about?" I drank more water and wondered for the thousandth time where Hawkins could be hiding out. I'd already checked the property at the edge of the Glades. The cabin too. The roof had caved in like I'd told my woman all those years ago it would.

"You know her," Luna stated.

Not wanting to think about that cabin in the woods, or the last time I was in it, I glanced at Luna. "Hawkins's old lady is dead."

Luna frowned. "How do you know that?"

Remembering that night seven years ago, remembering the sound of my elbow slamming into her face, hearing the cartilage shatter in my mind all over again—none of it made up for the fact that she'd pushed her own daughter off the porch. I wanted to kill her a hundred times over. More, I wanted to be free of the fucking grief from losing my woman. But every day dragged on like the last, and I didn't know if I ever would.

My head fucked-up, my mind in the past, I looked at Luna and I told him the fucking truth. "Because I killed her."

Luna's eyes went wide. "When?"

"Seven years ago." Seven long fucking years since I'd held my woman in my arms and watched her bleed out.

"And Hawkins knows this?"

Fuck, I didn't want to talk about this. "He was right there."

"What the hell happened?"

My jaw ticked, my nostrils flared, and I stared at my past. "She fucked up, and I elbowed her in the face. She died instantly."

"*Madre de Dios*, Hawkins didn't kill you?"

I leveled Luna with a look. "No. He blackmailed me into working for him."

Luna's shocked expression morphed, and suddenly he looked like he'd just solved the fucking puzzle of the century. "Jesu-fucking-cristo," he muttered, shaking his head. "It's true."

"What's fucking true?"

"Hawkins has a daughter. She lived out there with her madre."

"No." Hawkins didn't have a daughter. And I didn't have my woman. Not anymore. Seething, needing to get the fuck out of there, I stood and kicked my stool out of my way. "Had," I ground out, correcting Luna. "He *had* a daughter. She's fucking dead too. Hawkins and his old lady killed her."

I didn't wait for Luna to say shit.

I walked out of the bar.

Chapter
TWENTY-ONE

Candle

LUNA FOLLOWED.

"Hey," he barked. "I'm not here for me, pendejo."

"Then leave." I swung my leg over my Road King. "You're not doing me any favors."

Luna's right hand rested on a 9mm that was in a holster at his waist as he pulled out his cell phone with his left. "Aren't I?" His thumb swept across the screen then; he held his phone up to his ear.

I started my bike.

Glaring at me, Luna reached over and cut the engine. "Tyler, run a complete background on Stone Hawkins. I'm looking for any properties in his name, any businesses, and all past addresses…. Yeah. Copy that." He hung up and eyed me. "His daughter. She was your woman."

I didn't say shit. I sat there on my bike allowing him face time with me like a fucking tool.

"Amigo." Luna faked a look of concern. "What happened?"

"We're friends now?" Bitter, resentful, I threw my own damn impotent anger at him.

"Depends."

"Fuck off. I'm not having this conversation."

His expression turned all business. "You want to find Hawkins?"

"What the fuck do you think?" I'd been looking for him since I'd gotten out of jail.

"I'll find him."

"Because?" No one did shit for free.

"Because I offered, and I keep my word."

"What's in it for you?" He had an angle. "Besides the obvious of that piece of shit being wiped off the face of the earth."

"Let's just say he has a history of doing things I don't approve of."

"Like?"

Luna scanned the parking lot, then evaded my question. "You remember Hawkins's son."

How could I forget? The kid was a shit mechanic Hawkins had foisted on me before he set him up and threw him to the wolves over his bullshit with the cartel. As far I knew, my woman never realized she had a brother. "Yeah, I remember, but I didn't know he was his son until after he'd been working in the shop." Otherwise I would've told the kid to disappear when he had a chance. Now he was dead.

"Hawkins plays people like pawns, then disposes of them." Luna looked back at me. "He probably did the same to his daughter."

My jaw ticked. "I'm not telling you shit."

"You don't have to. I'll find him and tell you where he is. Then we'll be even."

And there it was.

"Even?" I asked, but I knew where this was going, and it started and ended with Kendall.

He scanned the alley on the far side of the bar. When he looked back at me, I saw it. The weight every man carried home from war. A lifetime of shit you wished you never saw or ever did but would do all over again in a heartbeat.

"You took care of Kendall," he finally said.

No one took care of that woman. More importantly, Luna wasn't thankful or even glad I'd shared time and space with her. He was looking for answers. "You're seriously still fishing?" He had it so bad for her, that trying to figure out whether or not I fucked her was eating him alive.

"Do I need to?"

I didn't relent. "Ask her."

Muscles tight as fuck, he suddenly looked like he wanted to pound my face in. "I'm asking you."

For the first time in as long as I could remember, I fucking laughed. Then I started my bike. "Tell you what," I said over the loud pipes, "you find Hawkins, and I'll answer whatever questions you have, including the one you're about to throat punch me for." I'd tell him whatever he wanted to know—as long as it wasn't shit Kendall would be pissed about.

"Keep your phone close."

"Right." I scoffed. "I've been looking for him for weeks, but I'll keep my fucking phone close." I revved the engine and kicked the beast into gear.

Then I did what I'd never done in front of my woman because I'd been too damn inexperienced at the time.

I peeled out.

Chapter TWENTY-TWO

Candle

I NEEDED TO CLEAR MY HEAD, AND RIDING WAS MY SALVATION, BUT it was always a catch twenty-two. I couldn't ride without thinking of my woman.

All those years ago on that dirt road in an orange orchard in the middle of nowhere, she'd trusted me not to wreck the only form of transportation we'd had. As I shifted through the gears, I could almost feel her hands on my leg seven years ago, showing me what to do.

She'd been patient with me. More patient than I'd deserved. She'd also been a spitfire, but she'd been my angel.

And fuck, she'd ridden so goddamn carefree. I could still see her hair blowing behind her and the smile on her face when she'd had a bike between her legs. She'd looked so damn happy. Simple shit had always brought her joy.

I wished for the millionth time that I hadn't thrown away my time with her. I'd been so focused on getting in the Rangers and learning skills I thought would help me take down River Stephens that I'd been fucking blind to life.

There wasn't a single thing I'd learned in training or experienced downrange that led to River Stephens's death. I knew a hundred ways to kill a man with my bare hands, and yet the one thing, *one goddamn thing*, I'd neglected to take into consideration wound up being the fucking catalyst that brought River Stephens down.

Teamwork.

Except I wasn't a part of any team. I wasn't a part of anything, not even when I was in the Rangers. I was a goddamn island in my head, and the only person who'd ever made me feel like I wasn't, was dead.

It didn't take a truckload of guns for sale to bring Stephens down. It'd taken headcount, a shitload of armed men and, all right, two bulletproof SUVs and one of Stephens's own men to turn on him. But I'd been blind to the reality of the situation until the shit had hit the fan with Kendall, and all I'd had was headcount. The resulting shootout was a cluster fuck, but it got the job done, and Stephens was dead.

That left Hawkins.

I'd be a fool to ignore Luna's offer of help.

Two and half years wasted working for Hawkins as I tried in vain to get my guns stateside, all the while I bought into the bullshit in my head. I'd thought all I'd needed to do while I worked on getting my guns into the country was take down his men one by one and fuck his club all to hell. Or get a moment alone with him so I could pull the trigger.

I never got that moment alone with Hawkins.

He was smart enough to know I'd kill him if he left himself that vulnerable.

Downshifting, I pulled into a familiar parking lot and coasted to a stop before cutting the engine. For a long moment, I stared at the darkened building with the "For Sale" sign out front that'd been the one place besides the Rangers that I could get lost in.

The repair shop.

When I'd left the Army, Kendall had picked me up at the airport, and I wasn't home two fucking seconds before Hawkins showed up and said he needed me to run his shop. Not wanting to alarm Kendall, I'd told him I'd be there the next day.

Shaking my head at my stupidity back then, I felt my cell vibrate.

Knowing it was Luna before I looked at the display, because only a handful of people knew my number and no one called me, I swept my thumb across the screen. "That was fast."

"I don't fuck around," Luna stated. "Where are you?"

"Out."

"Meet me at your place." He hung up.

Starting the bike, I turned the Road King around and headed home.

Ten minutes later, I pulled into my driveway as Luna got out of his armored SUV, followed by his right-hand man and another guy I'd never seen.

Holding a laptop, he tipped his chin toward his right-hand man. "You know Tyler." He glanced at the other guy with inked-up arms who looked sinister as fuck. "This is Shade."

Not bothering to put my bike in the garage, I headed

toward my front door. "You brought two men with you to Daytona to talk to me?"

"Four." He scanned the street. "We had other business."

I followed his glance. Sure enough, another black Escalade was parked a couple houses down. Fucking figures. I unlocked my front door and walked in. "Lucky me." I hated his jarhead bodyguards. They all had attitude.

Luna went to my kitchen table, took a seat and opened his laptop.

Smiling like a fucking cover model tool, Tyler strolled in as if he owned the place. "Just like you said, Ranger. *Lucky you.*" He slapped me on the shoulder before sitting down next to Luna.

The Shade fuck didn't say shit. Closing the door, he took up position at the front window.

"So here's what we got." Luna typed on his laptop, then spun the machine around to face me. "Two satellite images." He toggled a key. "First one."

Tossing my keys on the table, I looked at the image, and my back stiffened.

Aerial shot. Hawkins's property in the Glades.

Not sensing my anger, Luna toggled the same key and another image popped up of the same thing. "Second image."

"They're the same damn image, not that it matters. I've been out there." Five fucking times over the past few weeks. "He's not there."

Luna shook his head. "Not the same image. Look closer."

I didn't want to look at the house my woman had died

in. I wanted to burn it the fuck down. Why I didn't when I was there, I didn't know. "I fucking looked."

"There." Luna pointed. "What do you see?"

A bad fucking memory. "A shithole."

He pointed again. "Right there." He toggled back to the first image. "Now look at this one taken the day before yesterday."

I frowned. "Go back."

Luna switched to the second image.

He was right. It wasn't the same. "What the fuck is that?" The satellite image was grainy as hell.

Luna's shrewd gaze cut from the screen to me. "A bag of garbage."

A bag sitting right in front of the house that wasn't there any of the times I'd gone to check on the place.

The rage was instant, and I was moving.

Grabbing my keys, my saddlebag already packed with guns and plenty of fucking ammo, I aimed for my bike.

Luna stepped in front of me. "Wait."

Chapter
TWENTY-THREE

Candle

"Wait." One hand on his piece at his waist, Luna put his other hand on my chest. "What'd they teach you in the Rangers?"

"Get out of my way." Shoving past him, I walked out of my house.

"You're not a one-man show," Luna called after me.

Fuck him. "You don't know shit about me." I'd always been a loner. Always would be. The one chance I'd had at not being an island, I'd fucked up. This was my chance to even the score, and I wasn't letting it slip away.

"I don't give a fuck if you die," Luna warned.

"Good." I swung my leg over my bike. "Feeling's mutual."

"But Kendall does," Luna clipped as his two lackeys stood behind him.

Ignoring him, I started my bike.

Raising his voice, Luna strode toward me. "You got one single person on this earth who gives a fuck if you live or die. You think she'd want you to go there alone?"

I spared him a glance. "You're ignorant as hell if you think that's gonna have any effect on me. And the fact that you spewed that shit only tells me you don't know her at all. Good fucking luck to you." I kicked my bike into gear.

Fast as hell, Luna drew.

Without an ounce of humor, I laughed. "Shoot, motherfucker. I dare you."

Glaring at me for a moment, Luna shook his head and reholstered his 9mm. "You're being irrational."

Luna didn't know what irrational was.

Living with the ghost of my woman's memory for seven years, working for the man responsible for her death just to protect another woman from the same damn fate—that was irrational. I should've killed Hawkins the second my woman died, but stupidly I hadn't. Consumed with grief, I'd killed his old lady instead, but that had been sheer fucking luck as I'd swung out in an anguish-fueled rage. Then, instead of exacting revenge on Hawkins, I'd fucking run to the recruiters. Grief-stricken, out of my head, I'd let them ship me off without making Hawkins and his men pay for what they'd done.

Those were all irrational decisions.

But this? Now?

I was being rational for the first time in seven years.

Swinging my bike around, I peeled out of the driveway.

I didn't even make it halfway down my street before one of Luna's tinted-out Escalades sped past me and slammed on the brakes.

Forced to stop or plow into the damn cage, I hit the brakes.

The second Escalade pulled up behind me, and Luna

threw the front passenger door open. Stalking toward me, not saying a fucking word, he held his phone out.

I knew who it was before I took the damn thing. "Not interested, Kendall."

"Candle," she stated dryly. "Gee. Great to hear your voice too."

"Wasn't me who called you, so save your breath."

"I wouldn't have to save my breath if I didn't have to talk you out of being stupid. Rip shooting you wasn't enough? You want to get plugged by Hawkins now? And for what? To save my honor because he let his pathetic MC losers come after me for River's money? Newsflash, you Neanderthal, I don't need saving and River is dead. Go home."

She didn't know about Shaila because I'd never told her. I'd never told anyone—Luna's wild guesses notwithstanding. "Tell your man to go home and leave me the fuck alone."

"Why do you think he's there in the first place, asshole?"

"Not my fault you pussy whipped him into running a fool's errand."

"Jesus fucking Christ, Candle," Kendall snapped. "Get your shit together!"

For the first time in a long time, I had it together. "You done?" Since she was the closest I had to kin, I gave her the courtesy of this conversation. But that was as far as it extended. "I'm hanging up unless you got something useful to say."

"How's this for useful, you dick. *Don't die.*"

I was over her and this conversation. "We all go sooner or later. Quit sending Luna to check up on me."

"What did you think I would do when you ignored my calls for weeks?"

"Get a clue." She was smart. She should've figured it out.

"You know what, Candle? I'm done giving a shit about you. Throw your life away for all I care. You've been fucked-up since the Rangers, and I don't even know what to say to you anymore. You told me all those years ago to get my shit together, but what about you? When the hell are you going to move on from being River Stephens's digger and stop letting the past have that kind of power over you?"

The Rangers didn't fuck me up. Stone Hawkins did.

But she was right.

I was giving the past too much power. Which was why I needed to get the hell down to the Glades.

Not bothering to respond, I hung up and tossed Luna his phone.

Looking resigned as hell, he caught it and shoved it in his pocket. "You want to ride with me or should we follow you?"

"Not your business."

"Kendall's business is always my business."

Cocksucker. "She tell you to say stupid shit like that, or did you come up with that all on your own?"

"Watch it," he warned.

"Or what? You'll shoot me?" I smirked.

"I just might, pendejo. Leave your bike and get in the Escalade. Your pipes will announce your arrival a mile before you get there."

I hated to admit it, but he was right. Sound carried in the woods. If Hawkins was there, he'd hear me coming before I'd have a chance to get a jump on him.

Hard SIN

But I still didn't trust Luna. "What's in this for you?"

Fucker just leveled me with a look, and in that moment, I had to admit, I respected him. I knew that look and I felt it deep. The Marines were in him same as the Rangers were in me. Hero complex, blood thirst, military-trained killer—call it whatever the hell you wanted, but once men like us picked up a scent, we were following it through.

"Fine." I swung my bike around and drove back to my house. By the time I grabbed my guns and walked out of my garage, one of the Escalades was in my driveway.

The tinted-out driver window went down, and Luna inclined his head toward the front passenger seat.

I got in and glanced in the empty back. "Where're your sheep?"

"Employees," he corrected. "And they're in the other Escalade."

The initial adrenaline from seeing those satellite images waning, I leaned back in the leather seat as he pulled out of my driveway. I'd never admit it to him, or anyone else for that matter, but I was fucking tired. I hadn't slept a full night's sleep in six months, and before that, I couldn't remember a dreamless night.

As we passed the other SUV at the end of my street, it fell in behind us.

I smirked. "I thought Marines traveled in groups. Safety in numbers and all that. You sure you want to risk driving in your overpriced ride alone with me to Miami?" I hazed.

"You thought wrong, and we're not going to Miami. We're going to the western side of the Everglades."

Crossing my arms, I grunted at the mention of the Glades.

Cutting west to get off the barrier island, Luna headed inland toward the highway. After we hit the on ramp, the other Escalade sped up and passed us.

We'd been going eighty-five in the left lane for a while when Luna spoke again. "Tell me what happened."

Except for that Fed Morrison and the recruiter, I'd never told a soul about my woman. Telling them hadn't saved her life, and neither would shooting my mouth off now. "No."

Luna glanced at me. "How come you never told Kendall?"

"Who says I didn't?" I challenged.

"Because she would've told me about it."

I snorted, not because he was wrong, but because he was probably right. She'd had a thing for the Cuban pretty boy since she'd first laid eyes on him. She also trusted him. I didn't trust a soul, but for some goddamn reason, sitting in this cocoon of a cage, for the first time I was wondering what the hell would happen if I did tell someone about Shaila.

As if sensing my moment of weakness, Luna played me like a pro. "At this point, what do you have to lose by telling me?"

Nothing was the short answer. Everything was the complicated one.

I looked out at the dark night flying past. Then I opened my damn mouth and told him the truth of the hard sins I carried every single day I drew breath.

"She was pregnant with my child and I never told her I loved her."

Chapter
TWENTY-FOUR

Candle

Luna took his eyes off the road for a split second to look at me. "Sometimes the words we never say are the most obvious."

A half grunt, half snort was my only response. I didn't fucking want absolution. I knew what I'd done. I knew my sins. I knew the hard truth of who I was and who I'd been.

Luna thankfully stopped talking.

Silent and smooth and nothing like a Harley, the Escalade flew down the highway like a damn land boat. I couldn't help but wonder what my woman would've thought about the ride.

She probably would've hated it, and the thought alone made me almost smile.

Having a sixth sense like some of the Rangers I'd met, Luna picked up on it.

"What?" he asked.

"Nothing."

One hand on the wheel, he rubbed his other across his

jaw. "All right. Fair enough. But know this. If Hawkins is down there, I'm collecting."

Christ. "Just fucking ask and put yourself out of misery."

He glanced at me. "Did you sleep with Kendall?"

I looked him in the eye. "Never."

His chest rose with a sharp inhale, but his shoulders didn't relax. "Why'd you give her the flower?"

Slumping in my seat, I tried to stretch my legs in a space two feet too short for me. "Why does it matter?"

"Because she feels guilty about it."

"Bullshit."

"Truth."

Damn it. "Her and I talked about all that shit years ago. She knows where I stand. Tell her to let it go."

Luna was quiet a moment, then he nodded. "Can I ask you something else?"

"I'm locked in your eighty-grand cage while you're pushing ninety on the highway. Ask whatever the fuck you want."

"Why join the LCs? Why work for him?"

"Meaning why didn't I kill Hawkins years ago." Good fucking question.

Luna didn't comment, he waited.

I stared out the window at nothing but darkness. "The easy answer is he had footage of me killing some of his men. He threatened to take it to the Feds. Florida has the death penalty. He also said he'd take Kendall if I did anything stupid. The hard answer?" I shook my head. I'd never admitted this, not even to myself. "If I wasn't working on a plan to take Hawkins down, to take Stephens down, if I actually killed both of them, what the fuck would I have left?" I turned to Luna like he had the answers. "My woman is dead. What the hell do I have if not revenge?"

"Life, amigo." Luna glanced at me. "You have your life." He focused back on the highway ahead. "Which is a hell of a lot more than all the brothers we lost downrange."

I hated that he was right.

Chapter
TWENTY-FIVE

Candle

LUNA PULLED OFF THE COUNTRY ROAD AND ONTO A DIRT LANE that was now more familiar to me than the memory of the old pathways through the palmettos and slash pines on the River Ranch compound.

Slowing the Escalade, he cut the headlights and made a call through the SUV's Bluetooth.

Tyler answered on the first ring. "Boss."

"Report," Luna clipped, scanning our dark as fuck surroundings. "I don't see you."

"We're less than a klick ahead of you, I saw you pull in. Shade and I did recon. One vehicle and two bikes in the garage. Five headcount in the house and one outside. Two are in the front room of the house. Another in a bedroom on the west side, another in the back bedroom. Hawkins is in the kitchen, and a sixth man is outside on patrol. He's circled the property twice in twelve minutes. All men are armed. Semiautomatics."

"Entrances, egresses?"

My leg bouncing, my trigger finger twitching, I palmed the small piece of carved wood I carried everywhere before safely shoving it deep in my pocket.

"Only one. Front door," Tyler answered. "But the back bedroom has a window big enough to get in and out of."

"Copy that." Luna glanced at his watch. "I want Shade at the back window, Collins on the garage, and Tank stays with our vehicles. You're with me and Scott, front approach. Objective is capture, not eliminate. Switch to comms. Two minutes."

My head whipped toward Luna. "Capture?" Was he fucking serious?

"Copy that." Tyler hung up.

Luna cut the engine then eyed me in the dark vehicle as he handed over a communication device. "Yeah, capture." He slipped his own comm into his left ear.

"You don't even know who the fuck he has in there with him." Neither did I, but I could guess by matter of deduction from the LCs who didn't ride with me to the River Ranch compound. Not that mattered. Whoever was in there would shoot to kill. Most likely spray us with bullets the second we breached. "We need to neutralize them before they take us out."

Luna reached behind his seat and came away with a Kevlar vest he dumped in my lap before pulling out a second one for himself. "I don't care who he has with him, they're all accessories. Hawkins has outstanding warrants, and we'll capture and hold until the Feds get here. Gear up."

Jesus fucking Christ. "You called the Feds?"

Luna slipped his vest on. "Not yet."

Then I still had time.

Without a word, I threw my door open. Leaving the comm and vest behind, I screwed a silencer on my piece.

"Scott!" Luna bit out in a hushed tone as he got out of the Escalade.

Ignoring him, I walked right past the second SUV as all four doors opened and Luna's men got out. I didn't give a shit that they were all armed, trained Marines, and an op with them would be like being back in the Rangers.

The problem was it wouldn't be a deadly op.

Muttering a curse in Spanish, Luna caught up to me and fell in step. "We have a fucking plan, Scott. Stick to the playbook or stand down."

"*You* had a plan," I corrected.

"Don't make me stop you," he warned, his men on our six.

Adrenaline pumping, ready to make Stone bleed out, I paused for two fucking seconds and turned on him. "You know the difference between you and me?" I didn't wait for an answer. "I wouldn't be having this bullshit conversation with you if someone killed Kendall. I would've already pulled the trigger." That was what I'd learned from my past mistakes—never hesitate. I should've killed Stone the second he'd stepped out of the house seven years ago.

His jaw set, his face grim, Luna nodded at his men.

I didn't care what the hell they decided. I could take six of Hawkins's men on my own with one goddamn hand tied behind my back. Covering the distance to the last bend in the road, I only paused long enough to sight the asshole out front.

A hand covered my left shoulder a split second before Luna spoke in a barely audible whisper. "Wait. Thirty seconds and Shade and Collins will be in position."

I wasn't waiting for shit. The asshole was stationary and in my sights. I had the shot now.

"Scott," Luna warned.

I pulled the trigger.

"*Jesucristo*," Luna cussed.

I was moving before the asshole dropped.

The dull thud of the body hitting the ground sounded a split second before I was clearing the porch steps and kicking the door in. The memory of the last time I was in this house burned into my brain, I knew the layout.

Already aiming for the couch, I fired two shots.

The two pricks in the living room were dead before they drew.

Luna was barking orders into the comm, shots were fired in the front and back of the house, and Luna and his men were breaching, but I was already down the hall, striding into the kitchen.

Seated in a chair, his gun on the table next to him, Stone Hawkins crossed his arms and smiled at me. "Do you know why you won't shoot me?"

Fucking piece of shit. My gun trained on his head, I didn't drop my aim. "Because I'm going to cut you instead and watch you bleed out. You can suffer just like your daughter did."

"Report," Luna demanded into his comm as he walked into the kitchen behind me.

"Clear!" Tyler yelled.

"Clear," another voice yelled back.

My gun steady in right hand, I palmed my knife in my left.

Hawkins laughed. "You cut me up, you'll never find out where she is."

Taken off guard for half a second, I paused.

Then I snapped the hell out of it. "I know where the fuck she is." I didn't, but it didn't matter. I wasn't playing into his bullshit manipulation tactics.

Hawkins cocked his head. "Do you? Really?" He shrugged. "Because I would've thought you'd have rescued her by now if you knew." He grinned. "Or at least paid her a visit."

"I don't need to visit her remains," I ground out. I'd buried enough bodies to last me ten lifetimes.

"How about her living flesh and blood? That, I would've thought you'd at least care about." He waved a hand between us. "Since you're so intent on this notion of revenge."

I surged.

"Scott," Luna clipped as I pressed my knife against Hawkins's throat and my gun into his temple.

"You sick son of a bitch," I seethed. "You let your own flesh and blood die right in front of you and you did nothing." My blade drawing blood, I pressed the knife harder.

Still smiling, Stone Hawkins dropped his voice to a conspiratorial whisper. "She's not dead."

"Bullshit." *Fucking liar.* "I saw her bleed out. Nothing's going to save your life now."

Stone lifted an eyebrow. "But did you really see her die?"

Sick and twisted, he laughed. "Or maybe you just thought you did. Maybe you were confused. Don't you want to know where she is?"

I drew my hand with the knife back.

"Wait!" Luna shouted. "Hear him out."

"Yeah, *hear me out*." Hawkins smirked. "Because I can assure you, she's not—"

I slit his fucking throat.

Chapter
TWENTY-SIX

Candle

"Madre de Dios," Luna muttered. "Now we don't know where she is."

I wiped my knife on his shirt. "She's nowhere. She's dead."

"Who was he talking about?" Tyler asked.

Ignoring them both, I looked under the kitchen sink.

"Boss?" Tyler asked.

"Drop it," Luna warned. "Any survivors?"

"Negative," Tyler answered.

Rubbing alcohol. Two bottles. That would work.

Grabbing them, I spared Luna a glance. "Get everyone out of here."

Luna nodded at Tyler. "Clear out."

"Copy that." Tyler touched the comm in his ear as he walked out. "Retreat."

Luna waited until he was gone. "My men's weapons were used here."

"So." What the fuck was he worried about? Three of the six men had bullets from my gun.

"You're not hearing me," Luna clipped.

I fucking heard him just fine. "Scrub the serial numbers, dispose of the weapons. Problem solved." Using one of the bottles, I poured rubbing alcohol on Hawkins, a rug and the wood floor.

"Is it?"

Dropping the empty bottle, I searched the kitchen drawers for a lighter or a match. "You got something to fucking say, Luna, say it." Prick.

"What if she's alive?"

Finding an old book of matches, I turned to glare at him and bit out two words. "She's not." But as I said them, I fucking hated the crush of hope already spreading through my head like a goddamn plague.

Luna lowered his voice. "Have you looked?"

My nostrils flared, and if self-control hadn't been beaten into me in the Rangers, I would've killed Luna on the spot. "Sitting in a pool of her own blood, her heart stopped. Paramedics paddled her, unsuccessfully, then called T-O-D. It doesn't get more dead."

Luna averted his gaze and nodded. But then he looked back at me, and I could tell I was going to hate what he said next. "Why would Hawkins say she was alive?"

I was right.

I hated his question.

In the back of my mind, I'd been asking myself the same damn thing since he'd said it. "Because he didn't want to die and he was a manipulative, conniving fuck."

"What was her name?"

I took a match out. "Why?"

"Seven years is a long time to stay underground, amigo." Luna paused. "Let me do a search."

"No." I lit the match and tossed in on the rug. Then I lit another and held it to Hawkins's shirt.

Luna stepped back, but he didn't argue his point.

Turning a burner on the stove to high, I tossed a hand towel on top of it and walked to the living room. Opening the second bottle of rubbing alcohol, I dumped some on each of the dead fucks, the couch and the rug. The fire in the kitchen starting to pick up speed, I lit a few matches and tossed them around the living area.

Allowing myself one glance at the area on the floor where my woman had died, I walked out.

His phone in his hand, staring up at the slash pines, Luna stood ten paces away from the house. "Trees could catch if the fire gets high enough."

I didn't care if the whole fucking swamp burned.

Luna tipped his chin over his shoulder. "The rest of the men are back in the SUV."

Curtains caught fire and flames lit up the front window. The same curtains my woman had moved to let me know she was safe.

Except she hadn't been safe.

"All I'm asking for is a name." Luna turned and faced me. "It can't hurt to do a search."

I never should've let her step foot in that house.

"One search," he reiterated.

"I don't say her name out loud," I admitted.

"Why not?"

I glanced at Luna. "She was mine." I didn't expect him

to understand that I was bonded to her. Everything about her was mine. "Her name, her memory, I own that."

The light from the fire illuminating his face, Luna nodded like he understood. "I'm not trying to take that away. All I'm saying is, if it were me, I would want to know."

That was the problem. I didn't want to know. I didn't want to find out if she had a gravesite. I didn't want a coroner's report or a police file or some damn news article to tell me she was dead. I didn't want to live that hell all over again.

I just wanted some goddamn peace.

But staring at the house where my woman had died, knowing the man who'd let her bleed to death was inside with a slit throat, I still didn't have peace.

I didn't even feel settled.

My chest tight, my anger barely under control, a thirst to pull the trigger—nothing had fucking changed. Hawkins and Stephens were dead. That hunter had dismantled River Ranch. The Lone Coasters were defunct, and I didn't feel any goddamn different.

Fuck.

Fuck.

"Shaila," I clipped, watching the house burn. "Shaila Hawkins."

Chapter
TWENTY-SEVEN

Candle

LUNA WAS DIALING HIS PHONE BEFORE HER LAST NAME LEFT MY mouth.

"I need a full background on Shaila Hawkins. Age…" Luna glanced at me.

"She would have been twenty-five this year."

"Twenty-five," Luna repeated to whoever the hell he was talking to. "Do a quick search, all the usual avenues. Her father was Stone Hawkins. Let me know what you find out ASAP, then run a thorough check after… Copy that." He glanced at his watch. "Ten-four." He hung up. "Five minutes. If there's anything obvious, we'll get a hit."

He wouldn't get a hit.

I stared at the flames as the bedroom in front caught fire, and I wondered if my woman would've wanted to see this.

"What was she like?" Luna asked, as if he knew what I was thinking.

"She was better than this."

"Shit luck who she was born to," Luna mused.

"I could say the same."

He glanced at me. "Did you know who your parents were?"

"The more important question is, did it matter. And no, it didn't." I wasn't sure how much or how little Kendall had told him about compound life, but every female over birthing age was your mother and there was only one Father. All of it was fucked, and none of it was worth repeating.

"I got lucky. Parents wise." Luna almost smiled. "Except mi madre still prays every day for my soul. Don't think she ever reconciled a sniper in the Marines wasn't shooting blanks."

His phone rang, and my heart jumped.

"Luna," he answered.

But then he didn't say shit.

For forty-seven seconds he held his phone to his ear and didn't utter a goddamn word.

My heart jackhammered, adrenaline spiked, and I started to sweat like I was downrange with a band of hajis on my six and I was out of ammo.

"Copy that." He hung up and looked at me.

Jesus fucking Christ. "Well?"

"Shaila Victoria Hawkins. Twenty-six. Born at Miami General. Parental custody taken away from the mother when she was age four, no school records except an online GED eight years ago, and no death certificate." Luna paused.

I was about to shoot him. "And?"

"She was arrested four years ago in a raid at the Hangman MC compound in Hialeah."

All the fucking air left my lungs, and shit went upside down.

For a split second I didn't breathe.

I didn't even blink.

"She's in jail?" *She's alive?*

Short and clipped, Luna shook his head. "Drunk and disorderly, swung at the arresting ATF agent, released on bail, charges later dropped."

Four years ago.

Four fucking years ago, she was alive.

Rage, nausea, disbelief, sheer fucking desperation, I managed two fucking words. "Clubhouse address."

Nodding once, Luna touched the comm in his ear. "Tyler, Shade, meet us at my vehicle. Collins, Tank, stay behind and monitor the burn. Call it in only if it spreads to the trees. Cover your retreat."

Not waiting to hear the rest, I was striding back down the dirt lane toward the SUV.

She was alive.

She wasn't dead.

My woman was alive.

My head fucked, my mind twisted and all I could think about was why the hell hadn't she gotten in touch with me? Stone knew where I was. Where the hell had she been all this time? At the fucking Hangman's?

Luna caught up to me. "What do you know about the Hangman MC?"

Bunch of pussy fucking losers Hawkins had ordered his LCs to stay away from. Now I knew why. "Nothing except they're about to die." If my woman was there, I was killing every last one of them.

"Scott," Luna warned.

I yanked the passenger door open of his SUV, but then I spared him a glance. "You know who the hell I am, and it's no goddamn hero. If you don't want to be a part of this, stand down."

"I'm not your fucking babysitter." Luna's hands went to his hips, and he sighed like he was fighting for patience. "That said, I made a promise to Kendall."

"I don't want, or need, your damn charity." And he was wasting my time. I'd hiked out of this fucking swamp before and I'd do it again. Stealing the first ride I came across, I could be in Hialeah in an hour, two, tops. It wouldn't be hard to find out where the hell the clubhouse was from there.

Decision made, I started walking.

"Jesucristo," Luna snapped. "Get in the fucking Escalade."

I turned and glared at him, but I got in the cage.

Ignoring his Jarhead flunkies in back, I slammed my door shut.

"Where are we going?" Tyler asked as Luna got behind the wheel.

"Hialeah," Luna clipped.

"War," I corrected.

Shade checked the magazine on his 9mm, then slammed it back home. "I'm in."

Chapter
TWENTY-EIGHT

Shaila

I FLOATED.

My wrists cut from the handcuffs, my stab wound smarting, my scab across my chest itching, I kept my eyes closed.

And bounced.

A voice whimpered something unintelligible. Maybe mine, maybe that girl Shaila's. Drug-hazed and head throbbing, I didn't know.

Big, crushing hands tightened around my waist and ribs. "Shut the fuck up, whore."

Shaila was dead.

I was Whore.

A chain clanked against the headboard as my arms were stretched beyond comfort, making the cuffs bite into my wrists.

The dirty biker fucking me groaned. Sitting on my filthy bed, straddling me over his lap as he faced me away from him, he held my waist in a vise grip and pounded my used, sore pussy.

"That's it, bitch." He grunted. "Fucking take it."

He bounced me harder.

A third hand grabbed my hair and twisted my head in the opposite direction of where my arms were chained to the headboard.

"Open your mouth," a less deep voice ordered.

I opened.

A dick was shoved in.

Gagging—from the rank smell, from the flash hitting the back of my throat—it was instinctual. My jaw clamped down.

The dick jerked out of my mouth, the hand left my hair and a slap rang out a split second before my head snapped sideways.

Pain lanced across my face.

"You fucking cunt!"

Tasting blood, bouncing harder, my chest vibrated and I heard a weak laugh.

Rough fingers dug into either side of my jaw with a merciless grip. "You think that's fucking funny?"

Everything was funny.

Sick funny.

Fucked-up funny.

Bouncing funny.

Grunting funny.

Drugged-out whore funny.

I smiled. "Fuck you."

The bedroom door flew open and slammed on its hinges just as a second slap made contact with my face.

Two shots rang out, piercing my ears, then two more.

Wet spray covered everything.

Then all at once, the hands left my waist, my body pitched forward, and the dick left my pussy. I hit the floor face-first. My T-shirt, wet and tacky, stuck to my torso as my arms pulled tight against the chain. Rolling to my back, the room filled with the scent of copper and gunpowder.

I opened my eyes.

With half his skull blown out, his mouth open and his eyes in shock, a dead biker lay next to me.

The laugh bubbled up, but then got stuck in my throat as a furious face appeared above me a fraction of a second later.

A face I'd dreamed about.

A face I'd prayed to come rescue me.

A face I'd given up hope of ever seeing again.

A face I'd sworn to hate.

Sucking in a shocked breath, the girl I used to be came traitorously rushing back.

"Tarquin?" I whispered.

The barrel of his gun pressed to my forehead.

Chapter
TWENTY-NINE

Candle

For two whole seconds, I couldn't fucking breathe.

My woman. Alive.

Alive.

And being fucked by another man.

The shock morphed and it hit me.

Rage.

Blinding, seething, gun shaking in my hand *rage*.

I hadn't even blinked. Killing the motherfuckers fucking my woman one second, the next I was on my knees with my gun shoved against her head.

"What. THE FUCK?"

Men yelled. Luna shouted. Guns fired. Bullets ricocheted all over the fucking hellhole.

My weapon aimed, I didn't fucking move.

I raged.

RAGED.

Her eyes unfocused, her drug-addled body wasting away, she looked up at me in confusion. "Wh-what are you—"

"*This* is what you've been fucking doing for SEVEN GODDAMN YEARS?"

Shaking like a strung-out junkie, she raised her handcuffed arms like she was going to touch me. "*Tarquin?*"

Recoiling at that name crossing the lips of this woman, I shoved to my feet.

"Scott," Luna barked. "Retreat. *Now.*"

Three bikers with weapons raised busted into the room from the adjoining bathroom that had a door to the hall.

I fired three shots in rapid succession. All the fuckers dropped, and I retrained my gun, aiming at the chain attached to her handcuffs. I fired once, and her hands, freed from the headboard but not the cuffs, dropped to her chest.

"*Scott*," Luna clipped.

The woman I knew seven years ago never would've let herself get chained like a fucking dog, let alone taken drugs.

"Coming." Disgusted, furious, I turned to leave.

More gunfire erupted from downstairs.

"Shade's holding position." Weapon ready, Luna kept his aim trained on the hall. "Back exit. Go."

I stepped over the dead bodies.

"Tarquin, wait!" she cried out.

My back rigid, my shoulders set, I kept fucking walking.

"Jeso-fucking-Cristo." Luna looked at me like I'd lost my fucking mind. "She's *handcuffed*. You're not leaving her here."

"You want her, you take her." My past was dead. My woman was dead. My whole fucking life was a goddamn joke.

I stepped into the hall as another piece-of-shit Hangman came up the stairs. Firing once, I killed him, but I no longer cared if I got shot.

"*Scott*," Luna barked. "Oh fuck, she's ODing!"

Goddamn overdosing.

Was I supposed to feel sorry for her?

Two more assholes came running up the stairs.

I aimed at them.

Taking in my drawn weapon and the dead biker on the floor, they paused.

Fucking pussies. They should've shot me. "Leave."

Stumbling over each other, they rushed back downstairs.

Coming out of the bedroom, Luna barked out an order. "Cover."

Making a crucial mistake, I looked back at him.

And fucking froze.

So fucking small, her hands cuffed, blood in her hair, she convulsed in Luna's arms and her eyes rolled back in her head.

Guilt hit me like an IED.

Hate and rage warring for purchase in my head, I suddenly doubted what I'd seen in that room.

"Move, move, move," Luna barked as another round of gunfire erupted downstairs.

Forcing myself to take my eyes off her, my training kicked in.

Taking lead, covering Luna, I shot two more bikers and got us the fuck out of there.

Carrying a now limp Shaila, Luna barked into his comm. "We're clear, Shade. Retreat."

Jogging toward the SUV, I yanked the passenger door open and got in. "Give her to me."

Unceremoniously dumping her on my lap, Luna reached

for his cell as he covered the front of the vehicle and got behind the wheel.

"Hospital," I ordered.

"Already on it." Luna plugged an address into the GPS and touched his comm. "Shade, report."

Weighing next to nothing in my arms, I didn't want to look down at her. "Where the fuck is he?"

Luna scanned the street behind us. "Ten seconds."

I glanced at the clubhouse as that fucker Shade casually walked out the front door with a gun in each hand. Not covering his six, strutting like he was impervious to getting shot, he got in the back of the Escalade.

Luna took off.

Shade leaned forward. "She dead?"

"No." I didn't fucking know.

"You sure?" the asshole asked.

I looked down.

Fuck.

Fuck.

An oversized T-shirt covered in blood her only clothing, her wrists cuffed, her face sunken, she looked worse than dead.

Luna glanced at her, then nodded at Shade. "Handcuff key in my kit behind my seat. Inner pocket. Grab it."

"Copy." Shade rummaged behind me, and a few seconds later he reached for her hands and undid the cuffs.

Her flesh under the metal restraints was raw and broken, and I wanted to go back and kill anyone still breathing in that fucking clubhouse.

I was also so goddamn irate at her, I wasn't even thankful

she was still breathing. *Jesus fucking Christ,* she'd been fucking those goddamn bikers. And she'd been high as fuck. Something she swore she'd never do.

Trying to contain my rage, I glanced down again and shook her once, but she didn't so much as twitch. "ETA?" I barked at Luna.

"Less than two minutes." Luna drove through a red light.

Fuck. "Her breathing's so goddamn shallow, I'm not sure she has two minutes."

"Copy that. Hang on." Luna floored it.

Goddamn it, she was going to die in my arms... *again.*

"Come on," I barked. At her, at Luna, I didn't fucking know which. All I knew was I couldn't remember a single thing I'd learned in the Rangers about field triage, so I shook her again. "Keep fucking breathing, goddamn it."

"Almost there." Luna took a sharp corner and pulled into a hospital's ER entrance.

Shade was out of the SUV, opening my door before Luna had come to a complete stop. "Tell them her heart stopped. You'll get her seen sooner."

Carrying her nothing weight, I rushed into the ER and barked at woman behind the admitting desk. "Her heart stopped. She's overdosing."

Five words and it set off a buzz of activity.

The woman behind the desk picked up the phone, nurses appeared out of nowhere, Luna strode in, and we were shuffled through security access doors to a private room. Taking a stethoscope from her neck, one nurse listened to her heart while another wheeled in a computer and a third started throwing questions at me.

They all ran together.

"Is this blood hers? What did she take? Any known allergies? How long has she been unconscious? Is she a habitual user? Was she sexually assaulted?…"

They kept fucking going, but they didn't do shit to treat her, and the last question set me off. Irate, I glanced at Luna.

As if knowing I was on thin ice, Luna nodded once and addressed the nurse. "There was a bottle of opiate painkillers near her when we found her. The blood isn't hers. She was initially verbal before she convulsed and lost consciousness. That's all we know."

The older nurse looked from me to Luna. "Are either of you related to her?"

My mouth opened and not a goddamn thing came out.

Luna hesitated. "He's her husband."

The nurse's expression shut down. "Go back to the waiting room and someone will come get you when we have news." She pulled a curtain, blocking Shaila from our view.

I reached for the fucking curtain, but Luna's hand caught my wrist. "Leave it."

My nostrils flared, but I couldn't even make a coherent threat come out.

"For now," Luna clarified.

I walked back to the fucking waiting area.

Then I paced.

A minute, an hour, I didn't fucking know. Luna sat with his phone in his hand. Shade showed up, stood against the far wall facing the entrance, and stared.

I kept fucking pacing.

Finally some fuck in a white coat walked through the double security doors and aimed for me. "Mr. Hawkins?"

"Yeah," I managed through my clenched jaw, hating the fucking name but not saying shit.

The jackass looked twelve. "We've stabilized Mrs. Hawkins, and she's awake now, but we had to pump her stomach." He dropped his voice. "I believe she's been sexually assaulted and held against her will, but she's refusing to speak about it. A representative from the police department is with her now." He cleared his throat. "Regardless of what she decides to tell us, she's been a habitual substance abuser for some time. We're running some tests now, but I'm advising she be admitted to a program as soon as she's released from here. Another close call and she may not be so lucky."

My jaw ticked. "What room is she in?"

Fucker glanced at my shirt, then at Luna. "Ah, respectfully, I'd advise you to go home for the rest of the night and come back tomorrow. Let her get some rest."

As if sensing I was about to lose my shit, Luna stepped forward, holding his hand out. "André Luna, Luna and Associates." He shook the jerkoff's hand. "Mrs. Hawkins is under our protection, and for reasons directly related to her safety, we are neither able to leave the premises while she is here nor leave her in her room unattended. We need to know what room she's in and when she'll be able to be released."

"Well, technically she can leave anytime, but she has some recent injuries—"

"We're aware," Luna interrupted. "Can she leave now?"

I wasn't aware of shit except the scene of her being fucked playing on repeat in my head.

The doc rubbed his hands together like he was fucking nervous. "Well, she's finished with her IV antibiotics, but I'm recommending a ten-day course to ward off infection, and we won't have the results of her blood tests until tomorrow to see if she's contracted any sexually transmitted diseases."

"But there's nothing life-threatening right now?" Luna clarified, not even blinking at the last shit the doc said.

"No, but I recommend she be admitted and stay at least overnight. She's going to go through withdrawal symptoms, and I—"

"Thank you, Doctor. Since she's not yet admitted, we'd like her released now. With, of course, any prescriptions she may need," Luna added, pulling out a business card. "And please call me tomorrow when you have the results of her tests."

"Right. Okay. Well, um, if you gentlemen will wait here, I'll confer with Mrs. Hawkins and see if she's in agreement… to all of this." Pivoting, he practically ran for the security doors.

I took a step to go after him.

Luna put an arm across my chest. "Wait. She'll be out in a minute." He pulled his cell out.

"How the fuck do you know?"

Luna looked at me dead-on. "She's addicted. She's not going to want to stay here."

"I'm giving it five minutes then I'm going in after her."

Holding his phone up to his ear, Luna nodded as his gaze drifted. "Talerco, I need you tomorrow. House call." He rattled off my address. "Female, twenty-six, substance abuser, minor wounds… Copy that." He hung up.

"You're taking her to my place?" What the fuck?

"You want to check her into a facility where any Hangman could make a couple calls and find her?" Luna countered.

Shade smirked as he stepped up next to me. "The few losers that are left won't go looking for her."

"You want to take that chance?" Luna asked me.

Fuck. *Fuck*. "No." But I didn't know if I wanted her at my place either.

Chapter Thirty

Shaila

My throat burning, the shakes setting in, everything hurt. I felt ten days past dead.

"All right, Shaila." The female cop stood. "I'm going now, but if you need anything at all, don't hesitate to call me. I can help you." Looking both sympathetic and detached, she patted my shoulder.

I did what I'd been doing the past half hour. I ignored her.

"Take care of yourself." Lady cop stepped around the curtain and left.

Nurse Ratchet walked in, followed by the doctor who looked like he hadn't started shaving yet.

"Well, okay." The teenage-looking doctor clasped his hands. "You have some gentleman waiting for you that would like to check you out. However, I am strongly advising we admit you."

Gentlemen? Yeah, right. "I'm checking out." No way was I staying here. I didn't give a shit if it was cops or another dirty biker waiting for me.

"Mrs. Hawkins—"

"What paperwork do you need me to sign?" I asked, interrupting the boy doctor. "And do you have any clean clothes I could put on?"

Frowning, the doctor glanced at the nurse. "Please get Mrs. Hawkins some scrubs and let's get her discharge paperwork ready." He looked back at me as the nurse left. "I'm prescribing a round of oral antibiotics. It's important you take all of them because the stitched wound on your lower abdomen is infected."

"Yeah, about that. It hurts real bad. Can you give me some pain meds? Oxy works. A month's prescription will do."

Boy doctor's frown deepened. "Advil will be sufficient for any wound-related pain you may still feel. We don't give opiate prescriptions to Emergency Room patients, especially not ones who come in having overdosed on them."

Fuck. I had a feeling he wouldn't, but I was shaking so damn bad, I had to ask. "Then I need somethin' else, Doc. You can't discharge me high and dry."

"That's why I recommended you be admitted, Mrs. Hawkins." Boy Doc gave me a judgy look. "Detoxification is a crucial part to the start of the recovery process from substance abuse. If you had been brought in a few minutes later, we would not be having this conversation. You had a very close call. Frankly, you're lucky to be alive."

"Where is she?" a deep, menacing voice asked right before the curtain slid back with force.

My blood ran cold. My frayed nerves jumped, and my heart slammed against my ribs.

I knew that voice.

My fucking soul knew that voice.

I looked up and everything stopped.

My heart, my breath, the spins, the entire fucking world froze as I laid eyes on him.

Tarquin Scott.

Here.

Sweet mercy, it hadn't been a dream. I hadn't imagined him in my drugged-out stupor.

I was staring at Tarquin Scott.

And every single inch of my body, every shattered piece of my heart, every aching bone, muscle and nerve wanted to reach for him.

I wanted it so bad I could smell him like seven years ago was yesterday. Pine and citrus blossoms, and earth and sun-touched skin, and man and musk.

But it wasn't yesterday, and I wasn't looking at a River Ranch boy who wanted to be a Ranger.

I was staring at a hardened man.

Unforgiving, lethal-looking—his cold, pale-blue eyes were staring back as crushing need to feel the touch of the boy he once was tormented me. My breath lodged in my throat and tears welled, but I didn't even blink.

Afraid he would disappear, horrified he was seeing me like this, devastated he wasn't mine, I drank up every inch of him like he was the last drop of salvation on earth.

Bigger, taller, tattoos all over his arms, the bulge of a gun was tucked into his waistband under his shirt.

Oh God, that meant...

Shit.

Shit.

The dead bikers were because of him.

He saw. *Everything.*

My mouth opened, to apologize, to beg for forgiveness, to ask why the hell he'd married someone else, but then his eyes narrowed in warning and nothing came out.

"She ready to go?" Tarquin snapped at the doc.

Suddenly, I didn't give a shit that he looked madder than the time I'd told him to kiss me. I didn't care about the ache in my chest suffocating me. I didn't care that he was real and alive and standing next to me. Seven years of useless longing, despair, and repressed anger boiled up and I found my voice.

Glaring at Tarquin Scott, I spit venom. "Don't do me any damn favors. You can just fuck right off with yourself." I forced myself to look away from his wrath. "Doc, I'll be admitted."

Chapter THIRTY-ONE

Candle

BELLIGERENTLY GLARING AT ME, SHE THREW DOWN ATTITUDE. "Don't do me any damn favors. You can just fuck right off with yourself." She turned toward the shithead doctor. "Doc, I'll be admitted."

"No, she won't." Like fucking hell she was staying here.

The suicidal doctor pasted on a smile. "If you'll please give us a moment?"

I pivoted and walked the fuck out. But I didn't leave. I went straight to Luna in the waiting area. "She's telling that doctor fuck she wants to be admitted."

His phone to his ear, Luna spoke to whoever he was talking to. "Call you back." He hung up. "For what?"

Fuck if I knew. "Drugs?"

Luna sighed. "Listen. Maybe—"

"She's not bleeding. She's awake and she's talking. She's not staying here." I didn't trust hospitals.

Luna shook his head like I was an idiot. "So now you want her at your place."

"Just deal with the doctor before he admits her," I demanded.

"You ever dealt with an addict before?" he challenged.

Goddamn it. "You're the one who said you were dumping her at my place."

"That was before we knew if we'd have any Hangman heat on her, and before I sent Shade back there to cover our tracks."

"My place is a fucking qualifying solution now? It's only good enough if she's in danger from some asshole bikers?"

"Listen." Luna held a placating hand up. "I just spoke with Talerco."

"I don't give a damn who you talk to." He needed to get his fucking hand out of my face.

Luna inhaled deep and let it out slow like he was fighting for patience as he dropped his hand. "Do you know what years of prescription pill abuse is going to be like to deal with?"

"Yes." No fucking clue.

Luna eyed me a moment, then he lifted his chin. "All right, fine. Follow my lead, and don't be a dick." Luna walked over to the woman at the reception desk. Smiling like he wanted to fuck her, he addressed her by the name on her uniform. "Miss Henderson, we need to get back to see Mr. Hawkins's wife again. Mind letting us in?"

She smiled at him like she did the last time he asked her to let me through the locked doors. "Of course, Mr. Luna."

"Thank you, chica." He winked.

I pushed through the doors and Luna followed.

"Remember what I said," Luna warned.

"Ditto." I pulled open the curtain to the area Shaila was in.

Luna walked around me and addressed the doctor. "We'll just be a minute. We need to speak with Mrs. Hawkins alone. It's an urgent security matter."

The doc looked at Shaila, but she was busy glaring at me.

"Right." The doc cleared his throat as he took in Luna's unconcealed piece in his waist holster. "Myself or the nurse will be back." Fucker couldn't leave fast enough.

Luna turned to Shaila. "Here are your choices."

Her angry gaze cut from me to Luna. "Who the hell are you?"

"André Luna. Luna and Associates is my security firm, and we specialize in personal protection. We brought you in here tonight. As I just stated, here are your choices. You can come with us to a secure location, or you can stay here, be admitted, and answer the police's questions about the men found dead in your room at the Hangman MC clubhouse. Be advised, if you choose the latter, we're leaving immediately."

"We?" she asked Luna as she nodded at me. "So he works for you?"

"Make a decision, Miss Hawkins." Luna ignored her question. "You have thirty seconds." Sparing me a glance, he tipped his chin toward the waiting area. "I'll be out front."

Shaila watched him go. "What bullshit. You can leave now too." She rolled to her side.

"I walk out now, I'm not coming back," I warned.

"Good for you."

Fuck this. I'd had enough. "Get up. We're leaving."

"In case you hadn't noticed, I'm in a *hospital*." She looked over her shoulder at me. "You don't just walk out." She turned away again. "You have to be wheeled out or some shit."

I whipped the curtain back, and a nurse was standing right there.

Startled, she stepped back, but then she took in my arms, my shoulders and finally looked at my eyes. "I've got some clean clothes, Mr. Hawkins."

Calling me Hawkins made me want to shoot her, but for the second time, I kept my fucking mouth shut about it because I wanted to get the fuck out of here. "We're leaving. Get her dressed."

"No, I ain't," Shaila called over her shoulder.

"You want to talk to the cops now or later? They're in the waiting room," I lied.

The nurse looked between us.

Shaila rolled to her back and gave me a challenging stare despite her body trembling. "You're so full of shit."

"Fine." Calling her bluff, I turned to leave.

I made it one step.

"Wait," Shaila ground out before snapping at the nurse. "Gimme those clothes. I ain't stayin' after all."

The nurse handed her the clothes, then glanced at me. "You can sign the release papers."

"Fine." Whatever got us out of here.

"Goddamn son of a bitch." Cussing like a Ranger, Shaila struggled to keep the hospital blanket covering her chest while she pulled off the old, bloodied shirt that was stuck to her hair.

Without thought, I moved to help her.

Pulling her old shirt off, taking the new one from her shaking hand, I put it over her head.

She flinched as my hands brushed hers, but she didn't say

shit. Eyes weary, mouth shut, trembling like I scared the fuck out of her, she quickly pushed her arms through.

Jesus fuck, she was thin.

My throat suddenly rough, my next words were low and hoarse. "Need help with the pants?"

Dropping her gaze, she shook her head.

I gave her my back and looked pointedly at the nurse who was watching me like she'd never seen a man before. "Where do I need to sign?"

The nurse cleared her throat. "Here and here." She held a pen out.

I scratched out a shit imitation of a signature because I'd never learned cursive.

She handed me a bottle of pills. "Here are her antibiotics. Let me grab a wheelchair and we'll have her brought up front. Hospital policy," the nurse added when I frowned at the mention of a wheelchair.

"Hurry," I ordered.

With a nod, the nurse took off.

I turned back around.

Feet bare, still shaking, Shaila had managed to get the pants on and was sitting on the edge of the bed, her legs dangling. "Where are you taking me?" Her arms across her stomach like she was going to be sick, she didn't make eye contact.

"My place."

She curled in on herself even smaller. "I don't think that's such a good idea."

A wave of anger surged, but I kept my voice even. "You're coming to my place until you dry out." Or get clean, or whatever the fuck else she needed to do. She reeked of alcohol, other men, blood and sweat.

She snorted, then gave me forced attitude. "Gee, I don't think your wife and kids will like that very much."

Wife and kids? "You still fucking high?" Who the fuck did she think she'd bonded herself to?

She didn't have time to answer.

The curtain pushed back and an older lady with a wheelchair was there. "Here we go," the woman said cheerfully as she pushed over to Shaila. "Watch your step as you get off the bed." She reached for Shaila's arm to steady her as she held her other hand out.

Unlike when I'd touched her, Shaila didn't flinch. She took the old woman's hand and got in the chair.

"All righty then, we're off." The old lady patted my arm before pushing the chair toward the exit. "Come, come, time to take your little lady home."

I followed them out.

Luna was waiting by the sliding doors but stepped outside where Shade was behind the wheel of the Escalade.

Luna opened the rear passenger door and smiled at the old lady. "Thank you for the help, ma'am."

"My, my, such gentlemen." The nurse pushed Shaila to the open door. "I think you'll be in good hands, missy."

Shaila snorted and muttered under her breath. "Not like I have a choice." She got in the SUV.

I climbed in after her.

Luna shut the door and got in front. Shade took off, and no one said shit as Shaila pulled her legs up and turned toward the window.

Chapter
THIRTY-TWO

Shaila

I don't know how I fell asleep with my head spinning and the shakes making my body tremble like it was fifty below and I didn't have a coat on, but I did. Detoxing with a living, breathing, angry Tarquin Scott sitting right next to me and God help me, I fell asleep.

Maybe it was because this was the nicest car I'd ever been in or because my body was shutting down from no pain killers, or maybe it was because for the first time in seven years, despite the look on Tarquin's face, I felt safe.

I didn't ask how Tarquin had gotten past Daddy.

I didn't ask if his life was in danger.

I didn't ask how long I was really going to stay with him.

I didn't even ask about his wife or kids again, not that he wasn't a complete ass when I had.

And most of all, I didn't mention how he talked different.

Everything about him was different.

Except his scent.

He smelled like my Tarquin, and that just made tears

well, so I'd shut my eyes and prayed for sleep like I'd used to pray for him to come and do exactly what he'd done tonight.

Rescue me.

But that rescue didn't feel good.

Nothing felt good.

I felt small and shitty and mortally embarrassed about my station in life when he had important-looking friends with fancy rides who strutted around with guns on their waists like they were saving the world. And all I wanted was some damn pills.

Thankfully I'd fallen asleep.

But now I was awake and the huge SUV was slowing down as the scary-as-fuck inked driver pulled into a driveway.

Feeling like a coward, I pretended to still be asleep.

"Talerco will be here first thing in the morning. I told him to bring her some clothes," the man called André said quietly. "Need one of us to stay?"

"No," Tarquin replied. "She in the clear? Our tracks covered?"

"Everything's handled," the driver answered.

"Copy," Tarquin replied gruffly as the vehicle stopped.

"Call if you need something," André said.

"I won't." Tarquin got out of the vehicle.

"Pendejo," André muttered under his breath.

The driver made a derisive sound.

My door opened and I fought not to flinch as big hands undid my seat belt, but then his arms slid under me and I panicked. Before I could protest, I was lifted and against his chest.

A gasp escaped, my eyes popped open, and it was instinctual. I bucked.

"Relax." Tarquin kicked the SUV's door shut. "I got you."

Overwhelmed by the scent of him, not knowing what to do with my hands, hell, with anything, I crossed my arms.

Holding me so tight it made my bones ache, he walked up the driveway of a house that was smaller than Mama's but nicer in every way. I was so focused on him, that it took a moment to realize what I was smelling, let alone hearing. I looked past the house, and sure enough, under the light of the moon, there it was.

The ocean.

"You have a house on the beach?" My voice catching, my heart broke even more.

"Yeah."

I didn't want to cry, I wanted to murder Stone Hawkins. But tears welled anyway, and suddenly I couldn't go in a house he lived in with his wife and kids that was so close to the sand I could reach out and touch the grains.

"Put me down," I choked.

He set me down and pulled keys out of his pocket before deftly opening the door and shoving it open.

I stepped back. "I can't go in there."

"Why the fuck not?"

I hated how he spoke now. I hated his anger. Most of all, I hated how badly my heart hurt. "I can't see… your life." I couldn't say wife or children. I just couldn't.

He looked at me like I was out of my mind. Then words of cruelty came out of his mouth that never would've crossed the lips of the man I knew years ago. "But I could see your fucking shit show?"

There was nothing I could say that wouldn't sound shitty, except for an apology or acknowledgement of him rescuing me, but this situation was so far beyond an 'I'm sorry' or a 'thank you' that I didn't even try to be nice. "I didn't ask you to come."

His nostrils flared, his jaw went tight and his tone turned lethal as he leaned menacingly toward me and dropped his voice. "And I didn't fucking ask to see what I did."

My arms already across my roiling stomach, I stepped back. "Just take me to a hotel." No money, no ID, not even a damn pair of shoes, I didn't know how the hell I'd pay for a room, but I'd figure something out. Sleeping on the stupid beach would be better than stepping foot in his house.

"Hotel," he ground out, as if he couldn't believe what the hell I was saying.

"Fine, motel." I didn't fucking care. "Give me a couple twenties and drop me off somewhere. I'll figure it out. But I don't need your damn charity beyond that." If he had a stupid house on the beach, he could afford a fancy hotel, but whatever, I wasn't gonna be picky. I needed alcohol, pills and a decade to sleep. Maybe a sandwich because I couldn't remember the last time I'd eaten.

Staring at me like I'd lost my mind, he straightened to his full height as his hands went to his hips. "Motel."

"That's what I said."

His jaw ticked, his chest moved with an inhale, and then it happened so fast I couldn't have stopped it if I'd wanted to.

He picked me up and threw me over his shoulder.

Pain shot from my stab wound and radiated, stealing my breath.

I didn't scream. I didn't even gasp.

I gripped two handfuls of his shirt as he strode into his house.

Slamming the door shut behind us like he didn't give a damn who the hell he woke up, he walked through a darkened living room and down an even darker hall before shoving another door open and striding past a bed.

Not stopping to put me down, he went straight for an attached bathroom, hit a light, and turned a shower on. Then he unceremoniously dumped me in front of it and barked out a command. "Clean up."

Before I could catch my breath or my equilibrium, he was out the door, slamming it shut behind him.

The room filled with steam, and I blinked against the bright light.

Then I looked around.

White tiles, white counter, fancy wood vanity, nothing leaking, fixtures with no rust, no grimy walls, no lingering scent of sweat, smoke and alcohol—no filth. Just… clean.

Eat off the floor clean.

It was the nicest bathroom I'd ever been in.

Hell, it was the nicest room I'd ever been in, and there were two big, white fluffy towels hanging on a towel bar, perfectly folded.

I didn't know whether to cry or praise Jesus, except I swore off the Lord years ago, so I didn't do either. I stripped down and got in the shower.

Sweet mercy, hot water. *Real* hot water. The kind that burns your skin if you want it to, not the tepid, sulfur-smelling crap I grew up on or the faintly yellow shit that came out of the rusty pipes at the clubhouse. Pure, hot, *clean* water.

I held my face under the spray and opened my mouth.

Then I drank.

And drank.

For a long moment, I forgot about everything. The years, the clubhouse, the bikers, the soreness between my legs, the pain from my wound, the shakes, my headache—all of it.

But I couldn't forget about him.

The man somewhere in this house who'd finally come for me.

Tarquin Scott.

But not River Ranch Tarquin Scott.

Army Ranger, married with kids Tarquin Scott.

The thought made me burst into tears, and then it was as if the flood gates opened.

I sobbed and I fucking fell apart.

Choking on despair, wanting to die, wanting to kill Daddy, wanting to kill Mama, I grabbed a bar of soap and I scrubbed every inch of skin like I could scrub my shitty, *shitty* life away.

Then I scrubbed some more.

When half the bottle of shampoo was gone, when the water started to turn cool, when my hands were so pruned they hurt, I got out of the shower and reached for the fluffy white towel.

It was the softest thing I'd ever felt wrapped around my body, and it made me cry harder.

I didn't know how I got the hospital clothes back on.

I didn't know how I managed to wrap the towel around my head.

I didn't know they made little rugs for bathrooms that were softer than any bed I'd ever slept on.

All I knew was that I couldn't live like this. Curled in a ball, shaking from withdrawal and grief, I laid down on the rug and prayed to a God I no longer believed in.

I prayed for sleep to take me, and I prayed to never wake up.

Then I prayed to die here because it was the nicest place I'd ever been.

Chapter

THIRTY-THREE

Candle

I STOOD OUTSIDE THE DOOR AND LISTENED TO HER CRY.

Not cry.

Fucking sob.

I wanted to punch something, then kill Hawkins all over again. Feeling fucking impotent, I walked away like a goddamn coward. Going straight for the whiskey I kept in a kitchen cupboard, I had the bottle in my hand before I thought twice.

"Fuck." I put the bottle back and grabbed a water out of the fridge.

Downing it in one go, I realized she was probably thirsty. And starving, literally. Feeling fucking guilty, I looked in the fridge and spent the next twenty minutes making eggs and toast. Plating the food, I grabbed a water for her and went back to the spare bedroom. The shower off, no sound coming from behind the closed door, I stood there a moment and listened.

When I still didn't hear anything, alarm spread.

Dumping the plate and water on the nightstand, I rushed the bathroom and shoved the door open.

Jesus fucking Christ.

Curled in a small-ass ball, her hair in a towel, the shit hospital clothes on, she was asleep.

For two crushing minutes, I stood there and stared.

My whole goddamn life, not even when I buried my birth mother, I'd never cried.

But looking at my woman on the floor of the bathroom, practically seeing her veins and bones through her ashen skin, I wanted to fucking cry. I also wanted to go back and kill every Hangman MC who ever breathed.

The woman I'd left in the woods seven years ago didn't deserve this.

Addicted, starved, handcuffed, used like a whore and now lying on a goddamn bathroom floor like it was salvation.

Fucking hell.

Trying to be more careful than when I'd pulled her out of the SUV, I picked her up. This time, she didn't fucking stir. Limp like she needed to sleep for a damn week, she weighed nothing in my arms.

Not wanting to put her down, but still so fucking angry at her, I carried her into the bedroom and set her on the bed. Like she used to do in that cabin in the woods all those years ago, she turned to her side and reached out as if reaching for me.

My heart took another hit, and I wanted to lay the fuck down with her and forget every goddamn minute of my life since the woods. But I couldn't let her sleep what was left of the night without getting something in her stomach.

"Hey." I grabbed her thin-as-fuck arm and gently shook her. "Wake up."

Unfocused and lost, her eyes opened and she blinked. Then as if remembering everything that'd happened tonight, she flinched and moved back an entire foot.

Trying not to scowl, I picked up the plate and sat down on the bed. "You need to eat something."

She looked at the food, then at me, and her eyebrows drew together. "You cooked?"

A memory of her as she read to me late at night in that cabin all those years ago surfaced. Her voice was almost as soft now as it was then, and I wanted to go back in time and do every goddamn thing differently.

I handed her the fork. "Eat."

Pushing to a sitting position with some effort, like shit hurt, she took the fork, but she didn't take a bite. "*You* made this?"

"Yes, I fucking made it. Now eat." I set the plate on her lap.

She looked down at the food. Then she looked up at me with tears in her eyes. "There're mushrooms in here."

And cheese and onions. All the shit she said she missed when we were living in the swamp. But I didn't say that. Instead, I blurted out a hard truth. "I killed Hawkins."

For a long moment, she didn't react.

Then she dropped her gaze, forking a bite, and ate.

Chewing slowly, her eyes closed and her throat moved with a swallow bigger than the bite she took, like she was choking down a whole hell of a lot more than eggs, but she didn't say shit about her father.

"This is good," she said hoarsely, taking a second, larger bite.

I went for full disclosure. "I also burned down your house in the swamp."

Her chewing slowed and she swallowed. "It was never my house. Do you have something to drink?"

I opened the water and handed it to her.

She took a sip and gave it back before forking another bite. "The cabin?"

"Roof caved in. I left it alone."

She nodded, but she didn't look at me. "You learned to cook."

This wasn't the reaction I was expecting out of her. "I manage."

She didn't comment. She ate some more.

I couldn't tell if she was pissed, sad or indifferent. Selfishly, in that moment, I didn't care. I was sitting next to her and it was just her and me, and for one goddamn second, I wanted to pretend we were back in those woods.

But we'd never be those kids again.

"You need to drink all of this." My voice rough, I cleared my throat and handed her the water. "Stay hydrated."

"I drank some water in the shower."

She said it so casually, so matter-of-factly, that anyone else probably would've missed it, but I didn't. We'd both come from nothing. Clean drinking water was something most people took for granted, and after seeing the shithole I took her from, I'd bet my bank account she hadn't had access to water she could've drunk from a showerhead.

The thought fueled my barely contained rage, but I

shoved more shit down and kept holding the damn water out. "Drink more."

She took the bottle and our fingers touched.

Her eyes darted to mine, then just as quickly, she looked away and drank before handing it back to me. "Thanks. Tequila'd be better though."

This time I didn't keep my anger in check. "You're fucking done drinking. No more goddamn pills either."

She laughed, but it was forced and without humor. "I see you haven't changed much." She spared me a glance. "Except the way you talk."

A hell of lot more than just the way I spoke had changed. "Acknowledge me."

Sighing like she was put out, I saw a glimpse of the woman I used to know. "You think I wanted to be like this? You think I wanted to end up like my junkie mother?"

I didn't say shit.

Keeping her bloodshot eyes on me, she waited for a response. When she didn't get one, she shook her head and focused on the plate of food. "Damn it, this is weird. I look at you and I don't know you, but in the same breath, you're the most familiar person to me, except I can't even talk to you. I don't even know how to talk anymore. And lookin' at you… it just hurts." Abruptly setting the plate down, she turned her back on me and curled into a ball. "I need to go to sleep now. You can leave."

My hand came up, and for two whole heartbeats, it hovered over her shoulder.

I wanted to touch her.

Fuck, I wanted to.

I wanted her in my arms, and I wanted shit to be so fucking different, but all I kept coming back to was that goddamn clubhouse. I couldn't fucking scrub my mind of what I saw.

I wanted to unsee that shit more than I wanted to kill Hawkins all over again.

But I wasn't that goddamn lucky.

Picking up the plate, I walked out.

Chapter THIRTY-FOUR

Shaila

Drenched in sweat, shaking, the zaps making me twitch, I couldn't remember a worse night. Sweating through the only clothes I had, I'd somehow managed to rinse them out and hang them up in the bathroom, but now I was lying here, both freezing and burning up, and still sweating, and I didn't know what I wanted more, to die or just have one goddamn pill.

I was contemplating hurling myself naked into the ocean when Tarquin banged on the door.

Trying to keep my voice from shaking, I hollered at him. "I told you once, I told you a hundred times, I don't need nothin', and I don't want you comin' in here. I don't even give a fuck if the house is burnin' down. *Leave me alone.*"

Unlike all the other times last night when I'd gotten up and he'd immediately knocked like he was listening right outside the damn door, I didn't hear receding footsteps after telling him off.

Instead the door flew open.

"Knock, knock, wakey, wakey, sun's out, gun's out. Get decent, I'm comin' in." A blond man with green eyes and a smile that said he thought he was God's gift to women waltzed into the room. "Hey, darlin'." Ripped like he worked out all the time, he set a black bag with a red cross stitched on it down on the dresser. "I'm Talon. How ya feelin'?"

Pulling the sheet up around my chin, I looked past Talon.

Jaw locked, arms crossed, Tarquin stood in the doorway silently fuming.

Talon glanced over his shoulder, then backtracked a stride. "Doctor-patient confidentiality." He shut the door in Tarquin's face. Looking back at me conspiratorially, he winked and dropped his voice. "Always wanted to do that."

"You're a doctor?" He looked more like a surfer.

"Nope." He grinned. "But I was a Corpsman. SARC to be exact. Pretty sure I can handle anythin' you throw at me." He sat on the edge of the bed and dropped the pretense. "How are you really doin'?"

Southern accented, smelling like coconuts and beach, looking more like a magazine cover model than whatever he said he was, I didn't trust him. "I don't know what a Corpsman or a SARC is." And I didn't care, not unless he had little pills in his bag that would stop these fucking shakes.

"SARC is short for Special Amphibious Reconnaissance Corpsmen. I was a Navy Hospital Corpsman trained in advanced trauma management. I also did Force Recon training. Since the Marines don't have their own medics, I was attached to a Marine Force Recon Company. That's where

I met André Luna, the handsome devil you met last night. Although, he's not as good lookin' as me."

"You didn't serve with Tarquin?"

"Same war, different deployments. Didn't meet your boy until I was stateside." He put two fingers on the inside of my wrist and was quiet a moment as he checked my pulse. "Spoke with the attending doc at the hospital this mornin'. You want the good news or the bad news?"

"Seein' as I didn't ask you to come here, nor invite you in, how about you take your good news and your bad news and go out the way you came in." I tried to roll over, but he was sitting on the damn sheet.

Chuckling, he picked his kit up and dropped it at his feet. "Good news is you're gonna survive." His expression turned serious, and he looked at me pointedly. "Fortunate news is, besides the infection from your stab wound and your addiction, you're clean."

I didn't know what he was getting at. "Meanin'?"

"You don't have any sexually transmitted diseases."

Despite every ounce of moisture I'd sweated out, and the fact that I was shaking with withdrawal symptoms I wouldn't wish on anyone except the bastard who'd fathered me and those asshole Hangman bikers, I managed to blush. "Gee, how convenient seein' as I don't plan on ever havin' sex again."

His laugh was rich and soulful. "Oh, darlin', I am goin' to enjoy every moment of this. Mind if I pass that little tidbit along to the watchdog standin' outside this door?"

"Tell him whatever the hell you want. Tell his wife too. I don't care."

Talon frowned. "Candle has a wife?"

"Candle?"

"Tarquin," he corrected.

My heart caught in my throat. "You call Tarquin Candle?"

"That's his street name."

Bile rose, and I barely got the next question out. "What MC is he with?"

"Was. The Lone Coasters. There's nothin' left of them now."

Betrayal stole my breath, and for two heartbeats, I sat frozen in shock.

Then I rolled over and pulled my legs up. "You can leave now."

My stomach lurching, I wanted to grab the closest sharp object and go after Tarquin, that fucking asshole. I couldn't believe I'd been held hostage trying to protect him, when all this time he'd been riding with the LCs, *working for Daddy*.

Unaware of the last pieces of my shit life falling all to hell, Talon kept talking. "You said Candle has a wife?"

I choked back tears of rage and betrayal and shoved down every damn thing that I could. Tarquin didn't deserve my hurt or anger any more than he deserved an apology from me. For seven years, I'd fought to keep him safe, but he didn't do the same, so fuck him. I'd move on like he'd moved on.

Desperate for something to focus on, I answered Talon's question even though the last thing I wanted to do was talk about *him*. "I was told he did. But I haven't seen or heard anyone but Tarquin in this house since we've been here."

"Who told you?" Talon asked casually as he felt my forehead.

"My daddy. You can leave now." I wanted to stop thinking about Tarquin, but I couldn't help but wonder if he knew the whole time where I was.

"No can do. Not yet." Talon rolled me to my back and reached for the sheet. "I'm gonna look at that wound on your abdomen." Without consent, he lifted the sheet around my stomach and pressed on the sore spot. "Who's your daddy?"

I swatted at his hand and yanked the sheet back down. "You mean, who *was* my daddy. Stone Hawkins, and he's dead."

Like the flip of a switch, Talon went absolutely still and his expression shut down.

I snorted. "I see you've heard of him." I didn't wait for confirmation. The look on his face was answer enough. "Well, don't hold it against me, or do. I don't care. I can't control what anyone thinks. But I disowned that bastard a long time ago. Growin' up with him and livin' with a bunch of asshole bikers for the past seven years, I learned two things. There ain't no God, and no biker I ever met was worth a damn."

Shaking his head like he was shaking off a bad dream, Talon refocused and looked at me, but when he spoke, the casualness to his tone was gone. "Your man's a biker." Reaching for his medical kit, he pulled a bottle of Advil out and set it on the nightstand.

"Case in point, and he ain't mine." I nodded at the bottle. "I don't have a damn headache."

"Pretty sure we wouldn't be havin' this conversation if it

weren't for Candle." Next he pulled a bag of candy out and set it on the bed next to me. "The Advil will help. Six hundred milligrams every six hours."

"If I'd done a better job with my knife, we wouldn't be havin' this conversation either. So what's your point? Life's full of happenstance." I shoved the candy back at him. "I don't need any damn gummy bears." The thought of food right now made me want to vomit.

Talon gentled his voice and gave me a look I wanted no part of. "You stabbed yourself?"

"First of all, you can fuck right off with that shit. I don't need your damn sympathy or anythin' else for that matter. And second, not that it's any of your business, but I'm in no rush to repeat my actions. So cut the fake concern bullshit."

For one long moment, Talon stared at me and I stared right back.

Then he nodded. "Fair enough, but that wound still looks infected and your white blood cell count was elevated, so you need to keep takin' the antibiotics the doctor at the hospital prescribed."

"I don't have any antibiotics."

"Candle has them. He'll give you a dose today after you eat somethin'."

I smirked. "I can't be trusted with a bottle of antibiotics, but you'll set a bottle of Advil next to me?"

He raised a single eyebrow. "Can I trust you with the Advil?"

I flipped him off.

"How about the gummy bears?" He didn't miss a beat. "You trustworthy with those?"

"No. Take them away."

He chuckled, but then he sobered and his southern accent all but disappeared. "Opiate addition withdrawal is going to hit you in two phases. First phase you're experiencing now. Sweating, restlessness, agitation, muscle aches, and you probably had a hell of a time trying to sleep last night. Second phase can bring abdominal cramps, nausea, vomiting, chills."

"Oh trust me, I'm expcriencin' all of that."

"You can get through this," he reassured. "Watch TV, read a book, eat the candy, take a walk, stay distracted. This will pass. But also know there's no shame in asking for help or seeking a treatment facility or support group if you need it. You don't have to do this alone."

The thought of getting locked up in some facility made my anxiety ratchet to a whole new level. "With all due respect, fuck off."

A smile spread across his face, but it didn't reach his eyes, and his accent came back. "I hear ya, loud and clear. One more question, then I'll leave you to it." His voice quieted. "Do you want to tell me why you stabbed yourself?" He laced his fingers together. "Do you want to talk about any of it?"

Fighting for patience, I inhaled. "Look, I'm sure you mean well, but I'm not gonna wax poetic about bein' coerced to fuck bikers for seven years while my dear ole daddy told me I better do as he says or else. I took the fuckin' drugs they gave me, you're damn right I took 'em. I also spread my legs and drank every ounce of tequila I could get my hands on." I looked up at the man who was a complete stranger, but for some reason, since the moment I came to my senses in that hospital, Talon the SARC felt like the first person I could trust with the truth. "I ticked off days with my knife as a way of coping, but the day I stabbed myself was the day I realized I'd been there seven years and that ain't no kinda life. Seven years is the statute of limitations in a court of law, and I felt like I'd served my time. So I took that knife to my own flesh because I was high on drugs, and I didn't see no other way out at the time."

"And now?" he asked, no judgment in his tone.

"Now I just wanna get the hell through these shakes and sweatin' and cravin' for a damn pill I don't even want to take anymore, but my body hasn't caught up to my determination. Then once I get past all this, I need a job, my own place and to be left alone."

His hand landed on my shoulder and he nodded, but he didn't comment.

I appreciated that more than anything he could've said, and I was about to tell him as much when the door banged open.

"You've had enough time, Talerco," Tarquin growled. "Get the fuck out."

Chuckling like an angry Tarquin Scott standing in the doorway, rip-roaring mad, wasn't any kind of threat, Talon slowly stood. "She's all yours." Grabbing his bag, he winked at me. "Call me if you need anythin', darlin', but you're gonna be fine. Stay the course." He walked toward Candle but looked over his shoulder at me. "He has my number." Sparing Candle a glance, he grinned. "Ask her about her new resolution."

Glaring at Talon, Candle stepped aside.

Talon, that shit-stirrer, walked out.

Candle's gaze followed his retreat, then he looked at me. "What the fuck is he talking about?"

Pulling the sheet up, I closed my eyes. "Go away."

"No."

Christ. "Then shut up and don't bug me. I need to sleep."

"You need to eat and take antibiotics."

"You fuckin' eat." I picked up the bag of gummy bears and threw them at him. Or I tried to. No strength, my muscles hurting like I ran a damn marathon, the bag dropped in a pathetic heap a couple feet from the bed.

His gaze cut from the candy to me as his hands went to his hips. "I already did."

"Great. Good for you."

"Jesus fucking Christ." He stormed out.

I rolled over and prayed for sleep.

Chapter
THIRTY-FIVE

Candle

For five fucking days, I watched her suffer. I cooked, I sat in the damn hall outside her door, and I made her take the antibiotics. She wouldn't talk to me, and I didn't want to talk to her.

I wanted every goddamn thing to be different.

I hated who she'd become.

But as the days wore on, I hated her less for it and blamed myself more.

I was cleaning up dishes from another dinner she'd barely touched when I felt the air shift behind me.

I turned.

Standing where the hall met the living area, it was the first time she'd ventured out of the guest room. Wearing a tank and some legging things Talon had brought her, she looked better than she did five days ago, but she still needed a solid twenty pounds on her.

"Hey." I shut off the water and picked up a towel to dry my hands.

She looked around the living room and open-plan kitchen. "Nice place. Where is everybody?"

"Everybody who?"

She shrugged. "I dunno. Wife, kids."

The anger was instant, but I bit it back. "I'm not married, and I don't have kids." What the fuck? Did she not remember who the hell she was talking to or what I'd told her all those years ago? I'd fucking bonded myself to her. I'd made a goddamn promise, and I'd kept it.

Shock colored her cheeks, and she looked at me for a long moment, then she cleared her throat. "Ever?"

My nostrils flared. "You really want to have this conversation?" Five days of nothing but one or two word acknowledgments every time I asked her a damn question, and now she wanted to fucking talk? *About this?*

She crossed her arms over her stomach. "I don't know."

Fuck this shit. "I was bonded to you." I didn't know how to be subtle.

She flinched like I'd hit her, but she didn't say shit.

"You got something to say to that?" I challenged.

Her posture stiffened and all of a sudden her smart mouth came out. "What do you want me to say to that? I'm sorry I wasn't faithful?" She spit the last word out like it was poison. "Sorry I didn't keep pure as the driven snow for seven years? While you were what? Screwing LC club whores?"

I snapped, and the shit thoughts I'd been festering on for six goddamn days came roaring out like a detonated IED. "Did you enjoy fucking every goddamn dirty dick in the Hangman MC? Did they make you come? How many bikers did you fuck each week? Hell, every day?" I didn't wait for an answer. I threw the hand towel down and stormed past her.

Grabbing my keys and jacket, I headed for the door.

"Where are you goin'?" she demanded like she had a goddamn right to ask me anything.

"Out."

"Coward."

I froze in my tracks.

She didn't just call me a coward. She didn't spit the word out or yell it in anger. She said it calm as fuck, and that had me turning on her. "What did you just say?"

Tears welling, she defiantly held my angry gaze. "The Tarquin Scott I knew wasn't a coward. But whoever you are now? Walkin' away, sayin' cruel shit—you're a goddamn coward."

I'd never hit a woman in my life. But in that moment, I wanted to put my hands on her.

"Go ahead," she taunted, glancing at my fisted hands. "Do what you're gonna do."

"Watch it," I warned.

"Or what?"

We stared at each other.

"Fine." She threw her hands up. "*Leave.* Enjoy that privilege."

"You're not a prisoner here," I bit out.

"Yes I am," she threw back. "I'm a prisoner *everywhere.*"

I fucking lost it. "You fucked other men!" I roared.

"You became a Lone Coaster!"

Chapter
THIRTY-SIX

Shaila

His fists clenched, his body vibrating with anger, he looked ready to kill.

I didn't care.

Words I'd been holding in for days came pathetically pouring out like it'd make any kind of difference in my fucked-up life.

"I tried." My fist hit my chest. "I tried to be the bigger person. I tried my whole stupid life to be better. To live with one damn creed when everythin', and I do mean everythin', was fallin' down around me, and that was bein' the bigger person. I told myself so many goddamn times *'Do what Jesus would do, Shaila. Turn the other cheek, Shaila. Don't hold a grudge, Shaila.'*" Tears welled. "Do you know how *exhaustin'* that is? Do you know what it's like to always be the bigger fuckin' person?" I didn't wait for an answer from a damn grave digger. "It feels alone is what it feels like, and that ain't never good."

He opened his mouth to speak, and I held up my hand. "No, you don't get to talk. You get to fuckin' listen because

I'm done. I'm done doin' what I'm supposed to, and I'm done forgivin'. I hope my mama rots in hell for pushin' me off that porch. I don't care that she's dead. I don't forgive her. I also hope Daddy burns a thousand deaths of excruciatin' pain in hell then burns a thousand more. And I hope you feel fuckin' guilty for leavin' me like you did. I hope you regret every *second* you never came lookin' for me." I sucked in a breath, but I wasn't done.

"You and your stompin' around anger can go to fuckin' hell. Leave for all I care. I don't give a good goddamn what you do anymore, because when I get outta here, I'm gonna find the nearest piece-of-shit drug dealer, and I'm gonna get a goddamn fix of the first thing that'll make me not *fuckin' feel*, because I. Am. DONE."

"You think you're the only fucking person here who's suffered?"

Fury blazed bright in his eyes, and for a split second, I envied him that.

I envied his ability to feel something other than complete and total despair. But then I locked that shit down because he didn't get to have that kind of sympathy, not from me, not for what he'd done. "Oh please, Mister I-Served-In-The-Army and I'm A Ranger, tell me *all* about your sufferin'," I mocked. "Tell me how bad you had it for seven years of *livin'*." Infuriated at his bullshit, even madder at the fact that he'd taken up with the LCs, I spat the last word out at him like all of this was his fault. Because that's what I'd done for seven years. I blamed Tarquin Scott for not coming for me.

"You don't know shit," he seethed.

"Oh trust me." I laughed bitterly. "I exactly know shit, and I'm staring right at it."

Faster than I could blink, his hand was around my throat and my body was practically airborne as I was shoved against the nearest wall. "You want to know what I went through?" His veins on his neck popping, his jaw clenched, he bit the words out with a deadly intent I had never heard from him.

"Gee," I taunted, not letting him see the fear deep inside me, a fear I wouldn't even admit to myself. "Tell me all about your country club livin' on the beach."

"I have never, nor will I ever, step foot in a country club." His tone went suddenly, terrifyingly calm. "But I did step foot downrange. I fucking ate, slept, and breathed the special kind of hell that's reserved for a war zone. I fought, I killed, and I saw grown men beg for their lives after having their legs blown off, and they were the lucky ones. I pulled the fucking trigger so many times, I stopped counting the number of lives I took in the name of freedom. I saw carnage you can't begin to imagine, and I did this after watching my woman bleed out in my arms as she lost my child. Then I came back to this hellhole and worked for your blackmailing, piece-of-shit father because he not only held your death over my head, he dangled another life in my face. And I sure as fuck wasn't going to be responsible for another innocent person's death."

"Liar," I rasped as traitorous doubt crept in.

His nostrils flared with an inhale, and his voice dropped even lower. "I fucking did what your *daddy* said, day in and day out. I trained his useless bikers. I worked his goddamn shop. I rode with those fucking assholes who didn't know the meaning of brotherhood, let alone loyalty. I did all of that for three goddamn years, but I *never* took a single breath without thinking of you."

I opened my mouth to spit words out, but his hand tightened on my throat.

"I'm not fucking finished, woman. You think I was living? You think I was out getting my dick sucked day in and day out, pounding tequila and popping pills like it was fucking sport? I was keeping my goddamn head in the game because there was only one thing I was fucking focused on. Stone Hawkins and River Stephens dead. *That's* what I was doing."

Nostrils flaring, jaw ticking, he kept going. "I spent years, *years*, planning your father's and River Stephen's deaths. I didn't give a damn if I lived or died, but I sure as fuck wasn't going down without both of them being wiped off the face of the earth first. So if you want to call that *livin'*, then yes, that's exactly what the fuck I was doing." Easing off only to shove me one more time against the wall, he dropped his hand and turned away from me.

Irrational, self-righteous rage gripped me. "Is that supposed to make me feel sorry for you?" I yelled. "Dear ole daddy blackmailin' the great Tarquin Scott." Was I supposed to believe that self-serving bullshit story?

Grabbing a bottle of whiskey from the cupboard above the oven, he sneered at me. "Oh, now I'm great?" He took a swig right from the bottle.

My stupid addicted ass had my mouth watering at the thought of alcohol, and not just tequila but any alcohol. "Obviously not because you're too stupid to realize I'm bein' sarcastic."

Glaring at me, taunting me, he took another swig. "What the fuck else is new?"

Everything.

Everything was new.

That was the problem.

For seven damn years, I had a vision of my man in my head. I may have put him on a pedestal, and I may have made him larger than life, but he was still the Tarquin Scott I pulled from the swamp. His words were pure, his integrity was true, and his steadfastness was more reliable than the rising sun.

But this man in front of me, with his inked-up, overly muscled body and cuss words bleeding out of his mouth, he was nothing like the man I'd found in the Glades. Every edge of him was road hard, and there wasn't a thing I recognized about him except his eyes.

Colorless blue eyes I'd dreamed about every night for seven years.

Then with that first cursed breath I drew each morning I woke, traitorous hope filled my head with a single thought. Would today be the day? Would today be the day I finally saw him again?

No matter how hard I'd tried, no matter how low I'd sunk, no matter how many pills or how many drinks I'd poured down my throat, I couldn't stop those dreams and I couldn't purge that single, daily waking thought.

I'd hated it.

But I'd hated him more.

He'd left me, and if I needed to remember anything in this life, it was that.

Because the man I'd let walk away all those years ago? He wasn't a man who would've taken Stone Hawkins's word. He wouldn't have left my lifeless body alone. He wouldn't have walked away.

Tarquin Scott was a digger.

And my digger would've buried me.

Chapter
THIRTY-SEVEN

Candle

Hands shaking, eyes glued to the whiskey, she didn't utter another word.

Squaring her bony-as-fuck shoulders, she spun on her heel and marched out of the kitchen like she would've marched out of that fucking cabin in the woods.

Except nothing about her from back then resembled the woman who was currently slamming the door to the guest bedroom.

Her hair wasn't bright, her hips weren't full, her voice wasn't sweet and she'd fucked every goddamn biker from Hialeah to Belle Glade.

Motherfucking goddamn it.

I punched the old-as-shit cabinet. Then I punched it again.

It set off a chain reaction.

My fist pummeled the oak veneer, my rage grew exponentially, and splinters rained down on the fucking counter and floor as my knuckles smeared blood over everything.

I wanted to kill every fucking one of those bikers again.

Except I didn't want to just kill them. I wanted to rip their fucking guts out and shove them down their throats.

They'd fucked my woman.

And she'd been riding that goddamn biker like she'd been into it. *She'd let it happen.* But the woman I'd left in the woods never would've stood for that. She would've drawn her twelve-gauge and aimed at their dicks before she'd let them fuck her.

Enraged, I picked up the bottle of whiskey and smashed it against the counter.

Then I grabbed the next bottle out of the cupboard.

Out of my head, I took it by the neck and slammed it down on the edge of the counter like I was fucking christening my kitchen. The scent of alcohol burned my nostrils as blind rage momentarily blanketed the despair crushing my chest.

I grabbed another bottle.

Glass splintered, liquor soaked my boots, and I was reaching for the next breakable thing when the guest bedroom door banged open.

"Oh, that's rich," she spat our sarcastically. "Breakin' shit and makin' a dump of the place all because you pay the bills. How fuckin' self-indulgent and just like a man. Throwin' his weight around like he's worth all that."

"Watch it," I ground out in warning.

"Fuck you, asshole." In a sweatshirt two goddamn sizes too big for her, she stepped around me to avoid the broken glass and yanked a dishtowel off the oven door handle. "Grow up and clean your shit." She threw the towel at me. Then, just like a moment ago, she spun on her heel.

Except this time, she didn't go back to her room.

She headed right for the front door.

"Where the fuck do you think you're going?" I demanded.

Yanking the door open, ignoring my question, she stalked out and slammed it shut behind her.

I was going after her before I knew what the hell I was doing.

Wrenching the front door open, I yelled across my front yard at her. "*I said*, where the fuck do you think you're going?"

Not looking back, she raised her arm and gave me the finger.

Hell fucking no.

I moved.

Grabbing her from behind with one arm around her waist, I lifted her off the ground.

Kicking out, she pounded on my arm. "Let me go!"

"No." I started back toward the house, not giving a fuck if neighbors saw us.

"Put. Me. *Down*." She slammed her head into my shoulder the same time her elbow drove into my ribs.

My anger ramped up to a new level of fucked. "Did you fight those fucking bikers off like you're fighting me, or did you just spread your legs for them?" I couldn't stop the shit coming out of my mouth any more than I could stop the enraged thoughts in my head. "How about your mouth? Did you suck their dirty fucking cocks too? Swallow like a whore? How many of them tag teamed you, huh? Five? Six? What's your fucking limit for cock these days? One in each hand and one in each of your dirty holes all at onc—"

I didn't get the last word out.

Spinning in my arm like a woman possessed, she dug her fingers into my biceps and slammed her fucking forehead into my face.

My nose broke, blood spurted, and I stumbled. Tripping over a bush, I lost my footing and we both went down. My back hit the ground, and she fell on top of me.

Letting out a goddamn war cry, her fists started flying.

I didn't even think.

My training kicked in and I threw her off me.

But I didn't just throw her nothing weight off me.

I rolled and went in for the kill.

My body surging, one hand on her throat, I wrenched her arms above her head and shoved my knee down onto her chest.

She let out a forced rush of air.

Increasing the pressure, I fucking held her down.

Her mouth open, her face turning blue, she gulped for air like a fucking fish out of water. But my goddamn brain didn't catch up to my adrenaline. Dripping blood all over her, I squeezed her throat tighter with my bloodied hand.

"You think you can hurt me?" I seethed. "You think you have that kind of power over me?"

Her body uselessly fighting under me, she gurgled.

"Keep it up," I spat. "Keep fucking testing me."

Her eyes rolled back in her head and reality hit.

"*Fuck!*" Shoving off of her, I turned her on her side and barked out a command. "BREATHE."

She sucked in a labored breath.

Fuck. *Fuck.* "Another!"

Her chest rose, and she rasped through an inhale. Then another. After her fourth breath, she rolled to her back and our eyes locked. She lay there breathing, I sat there bleeding, and something shifted.

She shifted.

Reaching for my face, she did the one thing only she could do. She brought me back seven years.

"Your nose." She coughed. "It's bleedin'." Her thumb swept across my upper lip.

No woman had ever tended to me except her.

Not when I was a child, not when Kendall came to live with me, not any of the women I'd fucked around with since losing her, no one.

Just her.

For a split second the years disappeared and I wanted to slam my mouth over hers, but then in the next goddamn breath it was back—the image of those *fucking* bikers taking her.

Anger warred with disgust as I sat there frozen with her hand on my face. "Walk away," I warned, my voice off.

"Apologize," the fight gone from her, she still managed to make the word sound like a demand.

I'd never apologized in my life, and I wasn't starting now. "The day I apologize is the day you dig my grave."

"I'm not the digger, you are." Her voice dropped to a whisper. "But you never buried me."

I told myself to walk the fuck away. I told myself to bury the fucking past. I told myself she wasn't the woman I'd promised to take as my wife and I needed to let her go.

I told myself all of it.

But in the next instant, I was on her.

Slamming my mouth over hers, driving my tongue in, I didn't fucking kiss her—I thrust every goddamn ounce of rage I had into her.

Like no other woman on earth ever would, she wrapped her arms around me and took it.

Willingly.

Dissolving into me like she had no self, she took, she bended, and she made the distance of deployments, deceit, and despair disappear. But in the next goddamn second, I was tasting my own blood and the deluge of reality came flooding back.

The woman in my arms wasn't the pregnancy-swollen woman I'd left in the woods. This woman was drug-addicted thin and she'd spread her legs for who the fuck knew how many bikers.

I shoved her away and fucking spit on the ground.

Grasping at anger because it hurt so much goddamn less than grief, I threw accusations at her. "You kiss your bikers like that? You let them take your mouth whenever they wanted? Did you wrap yourself around them too?"

Shock widened her eyes before it morphed into hurt. Slamming her emotions down, anger contorted her face. "You think I wanted to do what I did?" Her voice pitched higher. *"You think I had a choice?"*

"You always have a choice." *God-fucking-damn it,* she'd had a choice. "No one was holding a gun to your head." Every fucking word I'd wanted to rage at her for a motherfucking week while she'd detoxed, surfaced with my mounting anger. "I fucking saw you in that club. I know what you used to be capable of. Handcuffed or not, you could've walked the fuck out, but you didn't."

Tears flooded her eyes. "I didn't have a choice."

Bullshit. "Yes, you did."

"He told me he would kill you!" she yelled.

Every muscle in my body went rigid.

My blood on her mouth, she choked on a sob. "Daddy said he would shoot you dead."

I blinked.

Tears fell down her face. "He made me do it. *He made me do it.*" Her hands covered her face, and she dissolved into sobs. "He kept me drug addicted like my mama. He shoved pills down my throat. He reminded me *every* week how he would kill you if I didn't do what he said." She choked on spit and tears and grief and anger. "He told me you had a wife. He said you had *babies*. Babies from a woman who wasn't stupid enough to ruin her chances of procreatin'." Her voice dropped to an anguished cry. *"He said you were happy."*

No air in my lungs, the fucking world stopped.

Then shit hit me like a detonating IED and I broke.

On my knees, *I fucking broke.*

Chapter
THIRTY-EIGHT

Shaila

His huge frame resting on his heels, his face dropped.

But it didn't just drop.

His expression went dead.

"That's why." I cried harder, pounding my fist against my chest. "That's why I didn't say nothin' when you found me. That look on your face right there," I accused. "Stop it. Stop it *right now*."

But he didn't stop it.

He didn't even see me.

His eyes staring right at me, he didn't see anything but what was inside his head, and the look on his face was a thousand times worse than the cruel words he'd thrown at me in anger. Blood in my mouth, anxiety in my veins, panic took me harder than ever before. Out of instinct, out of fear, out of desperation, I reached for him.

Shoving back and up, he rose to his feet without a word and strode to his garage.

"Tarquin." My neck sore, my body trembling, I scrambled to get up.

Hoisting the garage door open in one second, he was straddling a matte black Road King in the next. The engine roared to life, and he was backing out of the garage and down the driveway before I'd crossed his dirt-patched grass.

"Tarquin!"

Not even looking in my direction, he swung the bike around, revved the engine and took off.

I wanted to cry.

I wanted to rage.

I wanted to be so fucking angry that it didn't hurt anymore. But despair swept at my body harder than any drug ever could, and a truth I'd been pushing down for a week surfaced and I couldn't ignore it anymore.

I didn't hate him.

I didn't blame him for leaving me in the woods all those years ago.

I wasn't so stupid that I didn't see we were both victims of the same sick man. But that didn't take back the words I never should've said.

The truth was a death sentence for us.

I thought as long as he didn't know he'd been held over my head, as long as he didn't have to feel guilt for that, we might've had a chance. It's why I'd spent six days not saying a word to him. I never wanted to throw that burden on him, no matter how ugly things got. I'd been holding out hope that one day, *one day*, we'd find our way back to each other.

But now that hope was dead.

Tarquin wouldn't forgive himself.

And underneath all that Candle, he was still Tarquin. I saw the glimpse of the old him just now before he'd shut down, just as I saw the glimpses with every meal he'd fixed and brought me over the past six days. I saw it, and I'd crushed it as sure as I'd crushed any chance of a future.

My body aching, my soul too damn tired for my age, I forced myself to go inside.

The smell of alcohol hit me so fast and hard, I fell to my knees.

My hands shook, my body trembled, and I wanted a drink.

No, I wanted to escape.

I wanted to escape my head like I'd been escaping my life for seven years and drown in a pain killer, tequila cocktail. But irony's a willful bitch, and an unwanted, seven-year-old memory surfaced.

"He's gone," Daddy snapped. "Revive her and get her up."

"Sir, she's dead," one of the paramedics replied.

"Not my fucking junkie wife, you assholes, my daughter. Get her the fuck up. We need to go."

"With all due respect, sir. Your daughter needs the hospital. She's miscarried and she's lost a lot of blood."

Horrible cramping seized my stomach, and my heart wept at the word miscarried.

"She's not going to the hospital. Give her some pain meds and fix her the hell up like I paid you to," Daddy barked.

A cry slipped from my lips, and a large hand gripped my hair, yanking my head to the side.

"Open your eyes, girl," Daddy ordered. "Open them right now or I'm going after your River Ranch boy and I'm going to kill him."

I forced my eyes open.

A sick smile spread across Daddy's face. "That's it, girl. You're going to do what I say from now on. You know why?" He leaned closer. "Because I own you. I've always owned you." He stood back up to his full height. "And if you refuse to do what I tell you this time?" He yanked my hair and forced my head to look the other direction.

I cried out in shock.

With blood all over her face, her hair everywhere, Mama lay on the floor with her limbs splayed. No air filling her lungs, she was dead.

"That's nothing compared to what I'll do to your lover boy if you ever disobey me again." Letting go of my hair in disgust, he barked at the paramedic. "Get her the fuck up and make sure she's pumped full of pain meds."

Seven-year-old rage filled my belly, and I was pushing to my feet.

I was not going to be my mother.

I was not going to be Stone Hawkins's daughter.

And I sure as hell wasn't going to be pathetic.

I walked into the kitchen and picked up a towel. Breathing out of my mouth, I cleaned up every drop of alcohol and every piece of glass. I mopped the floors, I scrubbed the counters, and I took the trash out.

Then I showered.

My body trembling with remnants of withdrawal or anxiety or both, I climbed into bed and I waited. I waited until the clock ticked toward dawn and I couldn't hold my eyes open any longer.

Tarquin never came home.

Chapter
THIRTY-NINE

Candle

I drank until I passed out.

Chapter

FORTY

Shaila

"**Y**OU KNOW WHAT YOUR PROBLEM IS?"

Startled out of sleep, my heart slammed into my ribs and I scrambled back from the woman's voice.

"Awake now?" she asked sarcastically.

Gripping the blanket over my nakedness, I turned.

Tawny hair, matching eyes, sitting casually in the chair in the corner of the room with one bare leg crossed over the other, she was the fanciest woman I'd ever seen up close.

Raising an elegant eyebrow, she took me in like she knew everything about me. "Your problem is you don't know what you have."

"Who the fuck are you?" My voice sleep scratchy, the cuss word now ingrained, I sounded as trashy as I was.

Casually leaned back in the chair, a bustier pushing her boobs up like a perfect magazine advertisement for underwear I'd never be able to afford, she sat predator still.

"You don't even know who you are," she continued, like I knew what the hell she was talking about.

"Where's Tarquin?"

She smirked, and her perfectly painted, long, red fingernails tapped on the arm of the chair. "That's also part of the problem." She shook her head like she felt sorry for me. "He isn't Tarquin anymore." Uncrossing her legs, she leaned forward. "He hasn't been in a very long time."

"How the hell would you know?" I spat, hating her.

Graceful like a supermodel, she stood. "Because I lived with him for three years."

My stomach bottomed out, and a part of me that I didn't think could break any worse than it already had, shattered into irreparable pieces like a cruel joke.

"You fucked him," I rasped, my voice breaking.

All at once scathing and as pretty sounding as she was beautiful, she laughed. "That's another one of your problems. Blinding ignorance." She picked up the T-shirt I'd discarded at three a.m. while I was having the night sweats and tossed it at me. "Get dressed and meet me in the kitchen. We need to talk." In high heeled boots I never could've walked in, not even if you'd paid me, she turned toward the bedroom door.

"I ain't talkin' with you." Especially not about whatever she thought my *problem* was.

She spun and her icy gaze cut knowingly through me. "Do you know who Candle lets into his life?"

Two could play that game. I glared at her and her superior attitude.

"That's right," she continued as if I had spoken. "He doesn't let anyone into his life. And yet here you are, living in his house." She sauntered toward the door. "Get dressed and come to the fucking kitchen before I lose my patience."

I stared after her, not sure if I hated her attitude, her familiarity with Tarquin or her perfectly curvy body more. But damned if I was going to let her spend any alone time with Tarquin.

I threw on the T-shirt and went after her.

Self-righteous in my bedhead, morning breath and ill-fitting hand-me-down clothes, I walked into the kitchen like it was my own damn beach house. I still couldn't believe Tarquin had gotten himself a place that was spitting distance from the white sands. I hated that he had done it without me, but I hated it even more that the woman standing in the kitchen making coffee was more familiar with his house than I was.

"You seem to know your way around Tarquin's kitchen." Refusing to call him Candle, I glanced around the small living room, but he was nowhere in sight.

She did her superior smirk thing again. "Whose bedroom do you think you're sleeping in?" She filled the top of the coffee maker with grounds from the freezer.

"Not yours." I dished it right back. "This is his place." He'd said he'd never married.

She dumped the water in the coffee maker and put the pot underneath before hitting the start button with a blood-red fingernail. Turning to me, she crossed her arms. "You a junkie?"

Too close to home, the insult stung, and I lashed out. "Fuck you."

She shrugged. "Just asking, because from where I'm standing, you look like shit."

"From where I'm standin', you look like a slut."

"Better a slut than a junkie," she countered.

We glared at each other.

She broke first.

A smile, wide and sinister, spread across her face. "I think I like you."

"Well, I don't like you." Not one damn bit. "Did you fuck him?"

Her head cocked to the side as the aroma of fresh coffee filled the small kitchen. Her silky hair hanging perfectly away from her face, she looked like she'd just come from a fancy hair salon. "No, but I think you have. Which is seriously interesting because I haven't actually met any women Candle has fucked. His cock sucked? Sure. Okay, probably, but actually taking a woman to bed and sticking his dick in her? Never met one." She spun with a flourish as the coffee maker sputtered the last of the hot water out. "I used to wonder if he preferred men, but he did give me a flower all those years ago, so yeah…" She grabbed two mugs out of the correct cupboard. "Probably not gay."

You could have pushed me over with a feather.

This was her.

This was the woman who'd gotten him kicked out of River Ranch.

"You're from the compound." She was River Ranch.

"Don't sound so surprised." Two mugs of coffee in hand, she turned back to face me and tipped her chin at the breakfast counter. "We do exist. Name's Kendall by the way, nice to meet you. Now go sit your ass down."

I wasn't sitting down, and I wasn't drinking coffee with her, and I sure as hell wasn't taking her shit. Getting over my initial shock, I got down to the facts. "You almost got Tarquin killed."

She snorted as she perched gracefully on a stool. "He did that all on his own."

I hated everything about her. "Yeah, I'm real sure he meant to get himself stabbed and beaten for fun."

"Is that when you met him?" she asked casually before blowing on her coffee.

So she didn't know about me any more than I knew about her. "What business is it of yours?"

"None, unless you don't want to know what your problem is."

"I don't have a problem." I had so many, I couldn't count them all.

She laughed in earnest. It was shockingly pretty. "You got a six-foot-four problem."

"Why are you even here?" I demanded.

"I asked myself the same damn question the entire four-hour drive up here." She took a sip of her coffee. "But the chance to meet a mysterious woman Candle had holed up at his place was just too tempting not to come see," she said dryly.

"Gee, mission accomplished. Now you can go back to wherever the hell you came from."

"In case you didn't hear, River Ranch is dead. And did I meet you? I don't think I did because I didn't catch your name."

I was over her and her attitude. "Stay, leave, do whatever the hell you want. I don't give a shit," I lied. "I'm goin' back to bed." I spun on my heel.

"You're worried he doesn't love you anymore."

Like a moth drawn to a flame, I not only stopped, I turned back around. "Tarquin Scott doesn't love anyone."

"There's where you're wrong," she said all sing-song.

"I'm not talkin' to you anymore."

Screw her and the horse she rode in on. She didn't know shit about me or the years of hell I endured. I didn't care that she was from River Ranch or that she'd probably screwed Tarquin. As soon as Tarquin got back from wherever the hell he'd disappeared to, I was using his phone and calling that Talon guy and telling him to get me out of here. I didn't know where the hell I was gonna go or what I'd do for money to get there, but I was done staying here. Ain't no use beating a dead horse, and this place was exactly that.

Dead.

Everything here was dead to me.

The second I gave life to the thought, it was as if a switch flipped. The constant pain, the heart hurt, the despair, it all turned off, and suddenly I was left with nothing but a blessed numbness in its wake.

Maybe it was exhaustion, maybe I'd simply shut down, or maybe this was some kind of healing, but I took a breath and stared at the River Ranch Flower Girl. Then I realized something.

I didn't want a pill.

Or a drink.

I wasn't angry, jealous, mad or sad. I just... was.

Without another word to Miss River Ranch, I walked back into the guest bedroom and shut the door. My heart had shattered so many times over the past seven years, and I had so many broken pieces, maybe I didn't have any parts left to break. Maybe that was why I was suddenly so calm.

Whatever it was, I knew I was three lifetimes past normal and solidly into the fucked-up camp, but I didn't care. I'd never be able to compete with the prettiness of that Kendall woman, and I didn't fit in this house on the ocean with its fresh breezes and salt-scented air. And I sure as hell didn't belong cohabitating with a man who resented me.

And he did resent me.

I could feel it bone deep, and there was nothing I could say or do to change that. I couldn't undo where he'd found me or the seven years I'd been without him any more than I could change the weather.

I couldn't change a lot of things. But I'd gone six days with no drugs or tequila, not one dirty biker had touched me since Tarquin had killed 'em all, and I was alive and breathing—that was more than I'd had in the past seven years combined.

But what I didn't have was patience to sit around and wait for Tarquin to come back.

I opened my door and walked back to the kitchen.

Kendall raised a perfect eyebrow at me. "Change your mind about talking to me?"

"Do you have a cell phone?"

"Does a bear shit in the woods?"

Ignoring her sarcasm, I aimed for my goal, and damn it felt good having one. "Do you know Talon?"

She smirked then sipped her coffee. "Surfer, flirt, hot, irritating as shit when he's not playing God?"

That pretty much summed it up. "Yeah."

"Nope."

What the fuck?

"I make it a point to not know him," she explained. "I don't want to know what goes on in his head. But you? Call me intrigued."

"Do you have his number or not?"

"I better. I used to work for him. Now I generally avoid his coconut-surf-wax-smelling ass."

I held my hand out. "I need to call him."

"Are you dying?"

"No."

"Then I would recommend not calling him. Candle hates him."

I lost patience. "Phone. *Now.*"

She shrugged as she reached for a fancy purse on the counter. "Your funeral." She rummaged inside then handed me her phone.

I grabbed it and walked back to the guest room.

"The unlock code is six-six-six. You're welcome," she called after me.

I shut the door behind me. Dropping to the bed, I entered the code on her fancy phone, then I scrolled her contacts. When I got to 'Surfer Asshole,' I hit dial.

My nerves suddenly buzzing like a hive of bees, I listened as one, two, three rings sounded.

On the fourth ring, an accented voice like mine answered with a chuckle.

"Well hot damn, hell must've frozen over, because I can't think of any other reason why Patrol's woman would be callin' my sexy ass."

"It's not Kendall."

A second of dead air passed. Then, "I recognize this voice. Don't tell me Candle's in trouble again, because I'm not bailin' him out of whatever clusterfuck he stepped in. And trust me, he knows how to step in it."

"I'm not callin' for Tarquin."

All at once, Talon's voice turned serious. "You okay, darlin'?"

Inhaling, I sealed my fate at the hands of a stranger. "Can you come get me?"

He let out a long sigh. "Okay, I'm just gonna ask, because I had my heart set on spendin' the day with my women and I can guarantee you the last thing on my radar was rescuin' Candle's woman from him. All things considered, of course," he added. "So, that said, you injured or beaten? Or just runnin'?"

Appreciating his forthrightness, but prickling at the comment that he thought Tarquin would beat me, I kept my mind to myself about it and answered honestly. "Runnin'."

"Damn."

And that was it. That was all he said.

"Talon?"

"You do know you're checkin' all my boxes, darlin', right?" he asked as if he hadn't gone silent for a moment.

My senses tingled, and I wondered how big a mistake I'd made in calling him, but I didn't have any other options except the woman in the kitchen, and I didn't trust her as far as I could throw her. Not that I trusted Talon, but he hadn't lived with Tarquin. "Not sure I do."

"Southern accent. Damsel in distress. Pissing off Candle

Scott," he ticked off his list. "That's like a perfect trifecta, and I haven't even asked yet how you got Kendall's phone. I'm savin' that for dessert."

Ignoring most everything he'd said, I zeroed in on the one fact that could be a problem. "You don't like Tarquin?" He'd helped him by helping me.

The sound rich and full of life, Talon laughed. "Does anyone?"

I didn't answer.

He laughed harder. "Oh, darlin', now I'm definitely comin'. Gimme a few hours. You at his place still?"

I didn't have a few hours. Tarquin wasn't here now, and I didn't want to be here when he got back, let alone spend any more time with Kendall. "Where can I go to wait for you that's within walkin' distance of his house?" I hadn't seen anything out the windows but his yard and miles of beach since I'd been here.

His voice sobered. "You in immediate danger? Because Kendall knows—"

"I'm not askin' her for nothin'," I interrupted, losing patience. "I said I wasn't in danger. I just can't stay here any longer."

"Okay, darlin', I hear you loud and clear. Give me thirty seconds. I'm gonna make a call and call you right back. Talk to you in a few." He hung up.

The phone in my hand, I started to count.

Before I got to three, Kendall walked into the room and sat down beside me. "I heard," she said casually, checking out her manicure.

"Shockin'." Did the woman have no boundaries?

"In case you're wondering, nope, I don't give a shit about personal space or respecting your privacy."

"Uncanny," I muttered, willing Talon to call back sooner rather than later.

Ignoring me, Kendall carried on. "I'm just trying to figure out why the one woman who Candle loves seems to want to run away from him." Her gaze left her nails and zeroed in on me. "I mean, besides the obvious."

I was almost too afraid to ask. "What obvious?"

"That he's an asshole."

Her phone rang.

I glanced at it, then at her. I didn't want to talk to Talon in front of her in case she blabbed to Tarquin when he got back.

"Go ahead." She tipped her chin at her phone. "Talon sure as hell isn't calling for me."

"Do you mind?"

"Nope." She smiled and crossed her legs.

Turning away from her, I answered. "Hello?"

"Hey, darlin', it's me. I'll be there in about fifty minutes. I got a ride with wings. You good for an hour?"

I shifted further away from Kendall. "Um, I'm not really sure." I could go walk the beach and time it to come back in an hour.

"Oh, for fuck's sake." Kendall sighed loudly. "Give me my phone." Not waiting for me to hand it over, she snatched it from me. "She's fine. I'm with her." She nodded. "Yeah, yeah, yeah... I get it. I'm not fucking stupid." She rolled her eyes. "Right, sure, copy that or whatever you Army guys say." She held the phone away from her ear as Talon yelled.

"Marines, woman, MARINES."

She glanced at me and fake yawned. "Okay, got it, sailor. See you when your sorry ass gets here." She hung up.

Shit. "What did he say? Is he still comin' here in an hour?"

"Who the fuck is coming to my house?" a deep voice boomed.

I jumped, and Kendall sighed.

We both looked toward the door.

Wearing a murderous expression directed at Kendall, and the same clothes as yesterday, Tarquin's huge frame took up the entire doorway. "I asked a question. Who the fuck is coming here?"

"Well, well, well, look what the cat dragged in." Kendall smirked. "I see you're still silent as a mouse. At least you haven't lost all your skills." Lithe and graceful, she stood. "I'll let you two lovebirds talk. Or fuck." She looked between us and waved a finger. "Or whatever it is you two do together." She strode right at Tarquin and the only door out of the bedroom.

Chapter
Forty-One

Candle

What the fuck was Kendall doing here and what the hell had she said to my woman?

"I'll let you two lovebirds talk. Or fuck." Kendall waved her fucking finger between me and Shaila. "Or whatever it is you two do together." Smirking, she walked right at me.

I didn't move out of the doorway. "I asked you a question. Twice."

"Yeah?" She looked up at me with a half smile on her face as her hands went to her hips. "And I ignored it. *Twice*."

"*What* did you say to her?" My two pasts colliding, I didn't ask the question. I ground out the words in a demand.

"I told her you were an asshole and that you were in love with her. You're welcome." She shoved at my chest.

I didn't fucking move. "Tell me who the fuck is coming here, or I swear to God, I will lay a hand on you."

"And I'll lay you out. Go ahead, try me." Lifting a smug eyebrow, she crossed her arms.

"Who?" I barked.

"Talon," my woman whispered.

Grabbing Kendall's arm, I shoved her aside and stepped toward my bed. "You hurt?" Her arms around herself, her knees pulled up, her head was down.

"No," she said even quieter.

I spared Kendall a single glare. "Get the fuck out of here and don't come back."

Much louder, much firmer, and with much more attitude, Kendall gave me the same damn answer as my woman. "No."

I whipped my phone out and dialed.

Luna answered on the first ring. "Luna."

"Tell your woman to get the fuck out of my house in the next ten seconds or I'm going to shoot her." I put my phone on speaker. "Now," I barked.

"Jesu-fucking-cristo. Kendall, are you all right?"

"Peachy. But a strung-out woman wearing Candle's T-shirt doesn't look so hot. Maybe you should tell Candle to get the fuck out and stop scaring her."

"Five seconds," I warned.

"Babe," Luna clipped before lowering his voice and sounding worried as fuck. "What the hell are you doing there?"

"Four seconds," I warned.

Kendall ignored me and answered Luna. "After that phone call from him last night, did you think I was just going to go about my business today?"

"What phone call?" I didn't remember calling him.

"Scott, take me off speaker," Luna ordered.

I hit the button and held the phone to my ear. "What the fuck is she talking about?"

Luna sighed. "How much did you have to drink last night?"

A bottle of whiskey. Maybe two. I didn't fucking remember. "Answer my goddamn question, Luna."

"You called me at two a.m. demanding to know where Hawkins was buried."

What the actual fuck? "Why?"

Luna hesitated. "You said you were going to dig the body up and kill him all over again. My woman was in bed with me. She heard the whole conversation. She must've driven up there after I left for work this morning. In her defense, in her own way, she was probably just checking on you. She was worried, but she'll never tell you that. You know how she is."

I didn't give a fuck what Kendall was. But I sure as hell remembered wanting kill Hawkins all over again. I just didn't remember making that fucking call. So goddamn hungover, and feeling worse than when I'd been shot downrange, I made a decision I should've made the second I brought Shaila into the house. I was off the bottle. For good.

But none of that changed the past. Or the fact that I was so fucking irate, at Hawkins, at myself, at Kendall, at my woman, I couldn't see shit except red.

"Get your woman out of here before I do," I warned Luna.

"Copy that. Hand her the phone."

I tossed my phone at Kendall.

Catching it, she put it to her ear as she sneered at me. "Let me guess, you're going to tell me to come home and miss all the fun." She walked out of the bedroom.

I looked down at my woman.

Curled in on herself, she was so fucking small, it hurt to look at her. My chest ached, my mind raged, and all I saw day in and day out were those bikers on her. I didn't even give a shit that I'd killed them. It didn't undo what I saw. And it sure as fuck didn't feel like justice.

All I felt was anger.

At everything.

Calling on every skill I'd learned in the Rangers, I kept my voice controlled. "Why did you call Talon?"

Gaze averted, she rocked twice. "Because."

Fuck, fuck, fuck. "Pills?"

Her head whipped up and she looked at me with half disbelief, half anger, but she kept her tone even. "I'm done with all that."

She didn't look fucking done. She looked like she was crawling out of her skin. "Then why'd you call Talerco?"

She dropped her gaze. "Because."

"That's it? *Because*?"

"I don't need to give you a reason, Tarquin," she replied calmly.

"You sure as fuck do." She was in my house, on my watch, and she was mine. As fucked up as that sounded, I didn't give a shit. I wasn't gonna touch her, but that didn't mean someone else was either.

She looked up at me and spoke with the same damn calm voice. "Why do I need to tell you anything?"

My jaw ticked. My woman was never calm in an argument. "You're in my house."

"You didn't tell me where the fuck you were goin' when you disappeared last night."

I hated how she spoke now. "Language," I snapped.

She lost her bullshit calm and yelled. "Right back at you!"

My nostrils flared, my hands fisted, and I wanted to throttle the fuck out of her. I also wanted to hold her down and feed her. I hated her skinny-as-fuck frame. I hated her hair dull. I hated her cuss words. And I fucking hated the look in her eyes.

The same goddamn look I had in mine.

"Go ahead," she taunted. "Hit me."

Anger boiled to rage, and my fingers dug into my palms. "What the fuck did you just say to me?"

"I see your hands. I see your jaw. I know what men are capable of." She steeled herself. "Give it your best shot."

Like a fucking Ka-BAR gutting me, pain ripped through my chest. Then rage warred with guilt, and I barely got the next words out. "Is that what happened to you? They fucking hit you?"

Every goddamn day I saw the bruises on her neck that were barely fading. I'd been doing my damnedest to ignore them, to ignore all of it, including the reason for the antibiotic I had to give her every day. Talerco said she had an infection from a cut, but I'd never asked where.

"What do you care?" she spat back.

I fucking snapped.

Grabbing her by the arm, I pulled her to her feet and yanked my T-shirt over her head.

"What the fuck are you doing? *Stop it!*" Her movements too slow, she swatted at my arm, but I already had the shirt off.

Throwing it down, my gaze swept over her, and I went dead still.

Every inch of her was a mess.

Bruises on her thighs, her shins, her arms, her neck. Except it wasn't just bruising. Her hip bones, her ribs, her collarbones, all fucking sticking out, but that wasn't the worst of it.

Not even close.

A fucking slash wound cut across her entire torso, diagonally from her left shoulder to her right hip, ending at her lower abdomen where there was a raised red wound. The type of wound I recognized.

She'd been fucking stabbed.

Stabbed.

Dropping her arm, striding out of the room, I didn't stop until I was in the master bathroom, kicking the door shut behind me.

I threw the toilet lid up and I fucking vomited.

My stomach heaving, my chest compressing, I threw up every fucking ounce of whiskey I'd ever drunk.

The door banged opened. "You're such a pussy." Kendall pulled a towel off the rack and tossed it at me. "Pull it together."

Spitting out bile and the taste of puke, I flushed the toilet. "Get the fuck out of here." I turned on the sink and held my mouth under the tap.

"I wouldn't even have to be here in the first place if you weren't fucking up."

"I'm not fucking up." I was completely fucking up.

"Aren't you?" Kendall challenged.

"None of your business, D," I warned.

"Then whose business is it, *Tarquin*? Because you and I, we don't have anyone else who understands what we came from. Like it or not, we're each other's family. And guess fucking what? Family gives a shit about each other."

"I don't give a shit about you," I lied.

"Yeah, right," she scoffed. "Brush your teeth, pull your shit together and go talk to her before Talon gets here and takes away your choice to have a conversation with her."

"What the fuck does that mean?" That asshole wasn't stepping foot in my house.

"Exactly what I said it means. Why the hell do you think she called him? So they could go out to lunch? A movie? Hang like besties? Jesus Christ, for a Ranger, you're dumb as shit sometimes."

Goddamn it. "That's why she fucking called Talerco?"

"It wasn't for a check-up." Kendall casually inspected her nails like we were talking about the weather. "That girl has more pride than you, and that's saying something."

"Talerco isn't stepping foot in my house, and she's not going anywhere."

"Then go talk to her."

"No." *Fuck.*

"Why? What the hell are you afraid of? Shit can't get any worse between you two."

"You don't know what the hell you're talking about." The image of her bruised body tortured me all over again.

"Try me."

"Hell no."

"Do you want to lose her forever?"

Goddamn it. "You don't know how I found her."

She snorted. "You think André and I don't talk? You think I'm too stupid to put two and two together and figure out that the little handcuffed addict you all took from the gangbanging bikers isn't the same hot mess that's in the other room? So she's a little beat up and she screwed a few guys. So fucking what? If she was River Ranch, she would've fucked all the guys."

I glared at Kendall. "Not if I laid claim to her."

She crossed her arms. "You know that's not one hundred percent true."

"Yes, it is."

"Bullshit."

"Get the fuck out, Kendall."

"Oh my God." She rolled her eyes. "Get over yourself. You love her. She loves you. You're both hurting because you're both being fucking stupid." She threw her hands up. "But fine, don't listen to me. I'm done playing therapist. I'm not even getting paid for this shit." She turned toward the door.

"She lost our baby because of me," I blurted.

Kendall froze, but she didn't turn around.

"Seven years ago," I added. Then the hard truth started bleeding out of my mouth. "She'd found me in the woods after I was thrown out of the compound. Half dead, she dragged me from the swamp. She saved my life when hers was in danger. She's Stone Hawkins's daughter."

Kendall turned around. Eyebrows raised, eyes wide, she looked at me in disbelief. "No shit?"

Scrubbing a hand over my face, I nodded. "Stone was

going to sell her on her eighteenth birthday to some older biker in a rival club. I killed the asshole, and we hid out in the woods while I healed, laying low until her father stopped looking for us. The plan was for me to join the Rangers and get us both out of there. By the time I finally went to the recruiters, she was pregnant. I left her alone that day to visit her junkie mother in an isolated house in the Glades with a promise to be back that night to get her."

"Damn." Kendall slowly shook her head. "This isn't going to end well, is it?"

Steeling myself against the memory, I told her the rest. "While I was gone, her mother pushed her off the porch, and she miscarried. Instead of calling for help, her mother called Hawkins. He came and brought paramedics, but he withheld treatment from her until I got back. When I showed up, she was almost dead. I'd never seen anyone lose so much blood and live. Hawkins was waiting with armed LCs, all pointing guns at me. Then he blackmailed me into working for him. Said it was the only way he'd let the paramedics help her. I agreed, but it was too late. She flatlined. I held her in my arms, and I watched her die. Or so I thought."

"Jesus, Candle." Kendall sat on the edge of the tub. "So he faked her death just to get you to work for him?"

"I don't know if he intentionally faked it or if the paramedics got lucky and were able to revive her. I doubt she even knows what happened after she passed out. Anyway, I was in a rage after I thought I lost her, and I killed her junkie mother. Hawkins didn't retaliate, and I left, going straight back to the recruiters because I'd already struck a deal to enlist."

"Why didn't you kill Hawkins?" Kendall asked.

I scrubbed a hand over my face. "Because I fucked up." Because I was drowning in grief. Because I didn't know what to do. Because I'd lost everything I'd ever cared about. There were a hundred reasons, and all of them were shit excuses. There was only one hard truth. "I didn't take care of business."

"And you've been trying to make up for it ever since," she said perceptively.

I didn't say shit.

"I'm guessing you didn't know she was alive all this time."

"Not until a week ago. Hawkins was blackmailing her like he did me. Except he wasn't holding her over my head like he was holding me over hers."

"Oh fuck," Kendall breathed, suddenly making the connection. "Three years ago, when you came back for me, that was Stone that showed up at the house." She swallowed. "Did he know who I was?"

I nodded.

She pushed to her feet and stepped toward me.

I held a hand up. "Don't."

In a rare show of emotion, her face crumpled. "I'm sorry."

"I said don't. I made my own choices." I caught movement out of the corner of my eye and looked toward the open bathroom door.

"Kendall," Luna clipped, glaring at me. "Let's go."

Chapter
FORTY-TWO

Candle

"LET ME GUESS." KENDALL WIPED UNDER ONE EYE AS SHE smiled at Luna and gave him shit. "The surfer asshole is in the other room, you decided to come with him, and the Irishman brought you all here on his little puddle jumper."

"Chica," Luna chided, but his eyes softened when he looked at Kendall. "Roark is Scottish, I came with Talerco and Shade, and a nine-seater jet isn't a puddle jumper. Let's go. We're driving back."

Kendall scoffed. "I don't get to fly?"

Not sticking around to listen to their bullshit, I shoved past Luna. "Next time, don't fucking show up at my house and don't bring company."

"Next time don't call me at two a.m. belligerently drunk," Luna countered.

Ignoring him, I went to the second bedroom. Door open, room empty, I strode into the living room in time to see Talerco put his fucking arm around Shaila's shoulders.

"Hey, darlin', how you doin'? You keepin' it clean?"

My woman flinched slightly at the contact, or his bullshit. I didn't know which, and I didn't care. Both made me see red. "Get your fucking arm off her."

"Goddamn, Candle, I knew this was gonna be fun." Talerco grinned at me, then glanced down at my woman. "See? That's why I brought backup. Never can predict an angry Ranger." He squeezed her shoulder.

I stepped toward him.

Like a fucking choreographed Marine ballet, Luna and Shade appeared on either side of me.

"Stand down," Luna ordered.

I glared at the prick. "I will wipe the fucking floor with both of you if you don't get the fuck out of my way."

They both stood there.

"My woman, my house, my rules," I ground out.

Talerco looked down at my woman again. "Are you?"

"What?" Shaila asked, wide-eyed, glancing between me and Luna and Shade.

"Are you his woman?" Talerco clarified.

"I, um…" She bit her lip, but then she didn't say shit.

"Shaila," I warned, stepping forward. She knew who she fucking belonged to.

One hand going to my chest, the other on his piece at his waist holster, Luna stepped in front of me and lowered his voice. "Don't make a scene."

"So that's her name." Kendall smirked. "Southern and saucy. I like it."

My 9mm was in the fucking safe in the bedroom, but I had my knife in my front pocket. Glaring at Luna, I gave him one last warning. "Step the fuck out of my way, and I won't make you bleed in front of your woman."

Shade closed in, and I felt the telltale pressure of a barrel on my lower back. "You partial to your right kidney?"

"You partial to breathing?" Fucking asshole.

Talerco chuckled. "Yep, definitely fun." He steered Shaila toward the front door. "Come on, darlin', your chariot awaits."

Motherfucking shit. "*Shaila.*"

Her head down, she flinched when I yelled her name, but she didn't look up. "Don't, Tarquin." Small and scared, her voice cracked. "Just let me go."

Adrenaline pumping, alarm spreading, I shoved against Luna's arm.

Shade's barrel moved up my back. "You won't like having only one lung."

Fuck, fuck, *fuck*. "Goddamn it, Shaila, *talk to me!*"

Her hand going to her mouth, she covered a sob.

"It's been real, Ranger, but we're leavin' now." Talerco upped his pace and led her past me.

I moved.

The gun left my ribs. Shade kicked the back of my legs. I hit the ground, and Luna went in for an armbar.

On my knees, I grabbed the sleeve of my T-shirt and yanked it up. "Fucking look, Shaila! LOOK AT ME." One second, that was all I needed, *one goddamn second.*

Like I knew they would because she was my woman, her eyes cut to mine.

Luna's arm around my neck, Shade's gun against my temple, I didn't give a fuck. I held my arm out because she needed to see what the hell I was showing her. "What did you say to me in the swamp?" I demanded.

Tears fell down her face.

"*What did you fucking say to me?*" I jammed my finger against the two words I'd inked on my arm. "You told me to stay true." My voice broke. "*You said stay true.*"

Talerco spoke in her ear.

She cried harder.

I fucking lost it.

Throwing Luna off, I surged to my feet. "I stayed true, goddamn it. *I fucking stayed true.*"

Turning away from me, she choked on a sob, and Talerco opened the front door.

Roaring out the name of the woman I loved, I lunged. "Shaila!"

Pressure hit my neck, my legs gave out, and I dropped.

Shit went black.

THANK YOU!

Thank you so much for reading HARD SIN, the third book in the Alpha Antihero Series!
To continue the Alpha Antihero Series, and to find out what happens in the exciting conclusion of Candle's story, grab your copy of HARD TRUTH now!

The complete Alpha Antihero Series!
HARD LIMIT
HARD JUSTICE
HARD SIN
HARD TRUTH

Have you read the Alpha Bodyguard Series!
SCANDALOUS
MERCILESS
RECKLESS
RUTHLESS
FEARLESS
CALLOUS
RELENTLESS
SHAMELESS

Have you read the sexy Alpha Escort Series?
THRUST
ROUGH
GRIND

Have you read the Uncompromising Series?
TALON
NEIL
ANDRÉ
BENNETT
CALLAN

Turn the page for a preview of HARD TRUTH, the exciting conclusion to Tarquin 'Candle' Scott's story!

Hard Truth

I couldn't escape the hard sins of my past.

I couldn't unsee the truths in my mistakes.

Every breath she took was a reminder of the pain I'd caused.

Growing up at the mercy of a madman, I swore I would never give anyone that kind of power over me again. But here I was, on my knees, begging for a life I lost.

Except no amount of forgiveness would bring it back.

*HARD TRUTH is the fourth book in the Alpha Antihero Series, and it is not a standalone story.

The Alpha Antihero Series:
HARD LIMIT
HARD JUSTICE
HARD SIN
HARD TRUTH

About the AUTHOR

Sybil grew up in northern California with her head in a book and her feet in the sand. She now resides in southern Florida, and while she doesn't get to read as much as she likes, she still buries her toes in the sand. If she's not writing or fighting to contain the banana plantation in her backyard, you can find her spending time with her family, and a mischievous miniature boxer.

To find out more about Sybil Bartel or her books, please visit her at:

Website
sybilbartel.com

Facebook page
www.facebook.com/sybilbartelauthor

Book Boyfriend Heroes
www.facebook.com/groups/1065006266850790

Twitter
twitter.com/SybilBartel

BookBub
www.bookbub.com/authors/sybil-bartel

Newsletter:
eepurl.com/bRSE2T